W9-BBX-829

THE SEA OF GOLD

and Other Tales from Japan

Books by Yoshiko Uchida:

**The Dancing Kettle*
**The Magic Listening Cap*
Takao and Grandfather's Sword
The Promised Year
Mik and the Prowler
New Friends for Susan
The Full Circle
Makoto, the Smallest Boy
Rokubei and the Thousand Rice Bowls
The Forever Christmas Tree
Sumi's Prize
Sumi's Special Happening
Sumi and the Goat and the Tokyo Express
**The Sea of Gold*
In-Between Miya
Hisako's Mysteries
**Journey to Topaz*
**Samurai of Gold Hill*
The Birthday Visitor
The Rooster Who Understood Japanese
Journey Home
A Jar of Dreams
Desert Exile
The Best Bad Thing
The Happiest Ending
Picture Bride

*published by Creative Arts Book Co.

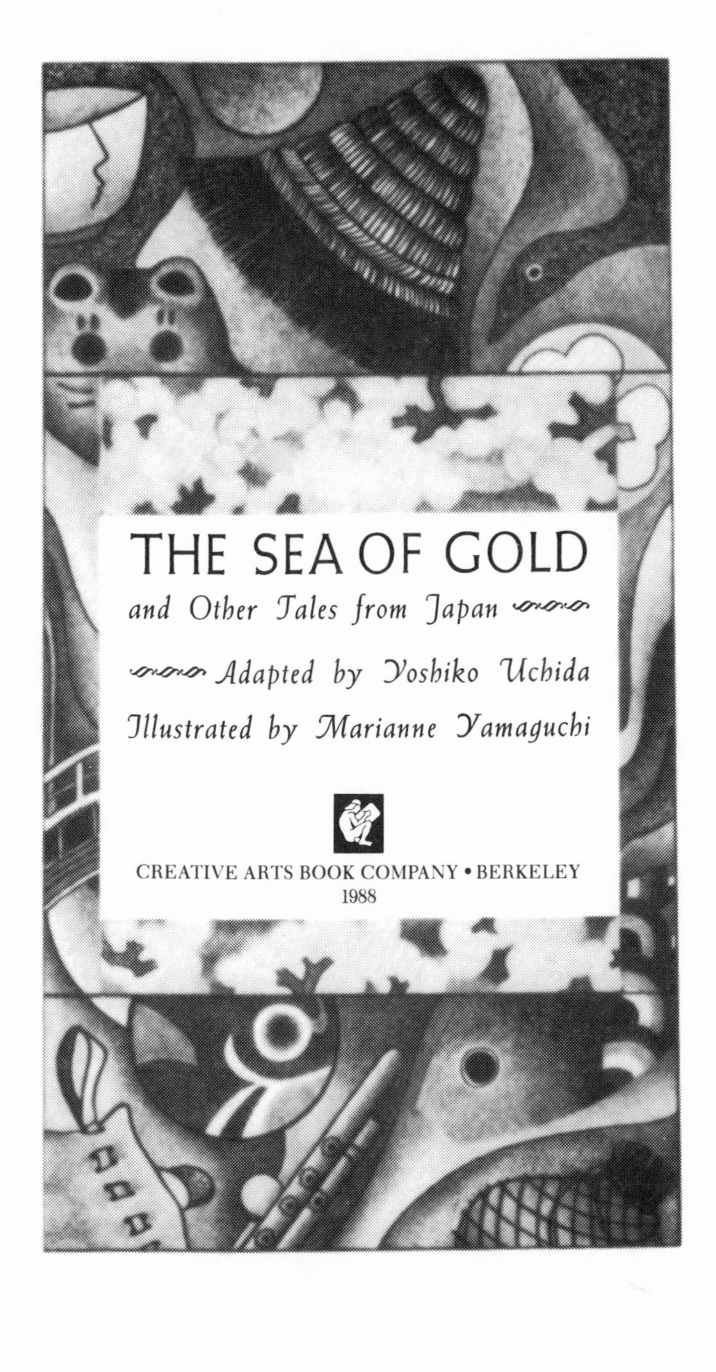

THE SEA OF GOLD

and Other Tales from Japan

Adapted by Yoshiko Uchida

Illustrated by Marianne Yamaguchi

CREATIVE ARTS BOOK COMPANY • BERKELEY
1988

ORIGINALLY PUBLISHED BY CHARLES SCRIBNER'S SONS IN 1965.
CREATIVE ARTS EDITION PUBLISHED IN 1988.

For information contact:

Creative Arts Book Company
833 Bancroft Way
Berkeley, California 94710

ISBN 0-88739-056-0
Library of Congress Catalog Card No. 87-72797

PRINTED IN THE UNITED STATES OF AMERICA

For Elizabeth, Robert,
Frances and Constance, Claudia and Emily

CONTENTS

The stories in this collection are folk tales which have been told and retold for hundreds of years to the children of Japan. Through the years, some stories have developed local variations, while others have become a combination of two or more familiar tales. All of them, however, contain the universal qualities which can be found in folk tales the world over.

I have not attempted to translate these stories literally, but have retold them in my own way as a teller of tales for the children of our time.

Y. U.

THE SEA OF GOLD

On a small island, where almost every able-bodied man was a fisherman, there once lived a young man named Hikoichi. He was gentle and kind, but he was not very bright, and there was no one on the whole island who was willing to teach him how to become a fisherman.

"How could we ever make a fisherman out of you?" people would say to him. "You are much too slow to learn anything!"

But Hikoichi wanted very badly to go to work, and he tried hard to find a job. He looked and looked for many months until finally he found work as cook on one of the fishing boats. He got the job, however, only because no one else wanted it. No one wanted to work in a hot steaming galley, cooking rice and chopping vegetables, while the boat pitched and rolled in the middle of the sea. No one wanted to be the cook who always got the smallest share of the boat's catch. But Hikoichi didn't mind at all. He was happy to have any kind of job at last.

The fishermen on his boat liked to tease him and they would often call him Slowpoke or Stupid. "Get busy and make us something decent to eat, Stupid!" they would shout to him. Or, "The rice is only half-cooked, Slowpoke!" they would complain.

But no matter how they shouted or what they called him, Hikoichi never grew angry. He only answered, "Yes sir," or "I'm sorry, sir," and that was all.

Hikoichi was very careful with the food he cooked, and he tried not to waste even a single grain of rice. In fact, he hated to throw away any of the leftovers, and he stored them carefully in the galley cupboards. On the small, crowded fishing vessel, however, there was no room for keeping useless things. Every bit of extra space was needed to store the catch, for the more fish they took back to the island, the more money they would all make. When the men discovered that Hikoichi was saving the leftovers, they scolded him harshly.

"Stupid fool!" they shouted. "Don't use our

valuable space for storing garbage. Throw it into the sea!"

"What a terrible waste of good food," Hikoichi thought, but he had to do as he was told. He gathered up all the leftovers he had stored and took them up on deck.

"If I must throw this into the sea," he said to himself, "I will make sure the fish have a good feast. After all, if it were not for the fish, we wouldn't be able to make a living." And so, as he threw the leftovers into the water, he called out, "Here fish, here, good fish, have yourselves a splendid dinner!"

From that day, Hikoichi always called to the fish before he threw his leftovers into the sea. "*Sah sah*, come along," he would call. "Enjoy some rice from my galley!" And he continued talking to them until they had devoured every morsel he tossed overboard.

The fishermen laughed when they heard him. "Listen to the young fool talking to the fish," they jeered. And to Hikoichi they said, "Maybe someday they will answer you and tell you how much they enjoyed your dinner."

But Hikoichi didn't pay any attention to the fishermen. He silently gathered all the scraps from the table and continued to toss them out to the fish at the end of the day. Each time he did, he called to the fish as though they were his best friends, and his gentle voice echoed far out over the dancing waves of the sea.

In such a fashion, many years went by until Hikoichi was no longer a young man. He continued to cook for the men on his fishing boat, however, and he still fed and talked to the fish every evening.

One day, the fishing boat put far out to sea in search of bigger fish. It sailed for three days and three nights, going farther and farther away from the small island. On the third night, they were still far out at sea when they dropped anchor. It was a quiet star-filled night with a full moon glowing high in the sky. The men were tired from the day's work and not long after dinner, they were all sound asleep.

Hikoichi, however, still had much to do. He scrubbed the pots, cleaned up his galley and washed the rice for breakfast. When he had finished, he gathered all the leftovers in a basket and went up on deck.

"Gather around, good fish," he called as always. "Enjoy your dinner."

He emptied his basket and stayed to watch the fish eat up his food. Then, he went to his bunk to prepare for bed, but somehow the boat felt very peculiar. It had stopped rolling. In fact, it was not moving at all and felt as though it were standing on dry land.

"That's odd," Hikoichi thought, and he ran up on deck to see what had happened. He leaned over the rail and looked out.

"What!" he shouted. "The ocean is gone!"

And indeed it had disappeared. There was not a single drop of water anywhere. As far as Hikoichi could see, there was nothing but miles and miles of sand. It was as though the boat were standing in the middle of a vast desert of shimmering sand.

"What has happened?" Hikoichi wondered. "Have we suddenly beached ourselves on an unknown island? Did the ocean dry up? But no, that is impossible. I must be dreaming!"

Hikoichi blinked hard and shook his head. Then he pinched himself on the cheek, but he was not dreaming. Hikoichi was alarmed. He wanted to go below to wake the others, but he knew they would be very angry to be awakened in the middle of the night.

They would shout at him and call him a stupid fool and tell him he was out of his mind. Hikoichi decided he wouldn't awaken them after all. If the boat was still on land in the morning, the men would see for themselves.

Hikoichi could not believe his eyes. He simply had to get off the boat to see if they really were standing on dry land. Slowly, he lowered himself down a rope ladder and reached the sand below. Carefully, he took a step and felt his foot crunch on something solid. No, it wasn't water. It really was sand after all. Hikoichi blinked as he looked around, for under the light of the moon, the sand glittered and sparkled like a beach of gold. He scooped up a handful and watched it glisten as it slid through his fingers.

"Why, this is beautiful," Hikoichi thought, and his heart sang with joy at the splendor of the sight. "I must save some of this sand so I can remember this wonderful night forever." He hurried back onto the boat for a bucket, filled it with the sparkling sand and then carried it aboard and hid it carefully beneath his bunk. He looked around at the other men, but they were all sound asleep. Not one seemed to have noticed that the boat was standing still. Hikoichi slipped quietly into his narrow, dark bunk, and soon he too was sound asleep.

The next morning Hikoichi was the first to wake up. He remembered the remarkable happening of the night before, and he leaped out of bed, ready to call the other men to see the strange sight. But as he got dressed, he felt the familiar rocking of the boat. He hurried up on deck and he saw that once again they were out in the middle of the ocean with waves all about them. Hikoichi shook his head, but now he could no longer keep it all to himself. As soon as the other men came up on deck, he told his story.

"It's true," he cried as he saw wide grins appear on the men's faces. "The ocean was gone and for miles and miles there was nothing but sand. It glittered and sparkled under the full moon and it was as though we were sailing on a sea of golden sand!"

The men roared with laughter. "Hikoichi, you were surely drunk," they said. "Now put away your daydreams and fix us some breakfast."

"No, no, I wasn't drunk and I wasn't dreaming," Hikoichi insisted. "I climbed down the ladder and I walked on the sand. I picked it up and felt it slip through my fingers. It wasn't a dream. It really wasn't."

"Poor old Slowpoke," the men sneered. "Your brain has finally become addled. We will have to send you home."

It was then that Hikoichi remembered his bucket. "Wait! Come with me and I can prove it," he said, and he led the men down to his bunk. Then, getting down on his hands and knees, he carefully pulled out his bucket of sand.

"There!" he said proudly. "I scooped this up when I went down and walked on the sand. Now do you believe me?"

The men suddenly stopped laughing. "This isn't sand," they said, reaching out to feel it. "It's gold! It's a bucket full of pure gold!"

"Why didn't you get more, you poor fool?" one of the men shouted.

"You've got to give some of it to us," another added.

"We share our fish with you. You must share your gold with us," said still another.

Soon all the men were yelling and shouting and pushing to get their hands on Hikoichi's bucket of gold.

Then the oldest of the fishermen spoke up. "Stop

it! Stop it!" he called out. "This gold doesn't belong to any of you. It belongs to Hikoichi."

He reminded the men how Hikoichi had fed the fish of the sea for so many years as though they were his own children.

"Now the King of the Sea has given Hikoichi a reward for his kindness to the fish," he explained. And turning to Hikoichi, he added, "You are not stupid or a fool or a slowpoke, my friend. You are gentle and kind and good. This gift from the Kingdom of the Sea is your reward. Take all the gold and keep it, for it belongs only to you."

The shouting, pushing fishermen suddenly became silent and thoughtful, for they knew the old fisherman was right. They were ashamed of having laughed at Hikoichi year after year, and they knew that he truly deserved this fine reward.

Without another word the men went back to work. They completed their catch that day and the heavily laden boat returned once more to the little island.

The next time the boat put out to sea, Hikoichi was no longer aboard, for now he had enough gold to leave his job as cook forever. He built himself a beautiful new house, and he even had a small boat of his own so he could still sail out to sea and feed the fish. He used his treasure from the sea wisely and well, and he lived a long and happy life on the little island where no one ever called him Stupid or Slowpoke again.

THE GRATEFUL MONKEY'S SECRET

There once lived a man named Kentsu who made his living by selling wine from village to village. Each day he carried two large earthen jars filled with wine and walked through the streets calling, "Buy some wine, some very fine wine! One drink and your worries flee, two and you double the length of your life, three and good fortune will be yours forever. Hurry now and buy some wine!"

Kentsu tried to think of all kinds of clever things to say in order to sell his wine, but often the villagers would ask, "How about yourself, Kentsu San? You must not be drinking any of your own wine, for good fortune certainly doesn't seem to come to you!" And it seemed so indeed, for Kentsu was one of the poorest men in the village.

However, Kentsu simply grinned and answered,

"I don't mind being poor at all." And he never grumbled because he didn't have any money.

Each day he rose early and hurried to the wine merchant of his village to buy his supply of wine. Then, carrying his heavy earthen jars, he trudged out toward the seashore. There he followed the curve of the beach, where the white foam brushed up to the sand, and he went from village to village selling his wine. His last village was at the foot of the distant hills, and if he was lucky, he sold the last of his wine there and came home with a light load and a cheerful glow.

One fine day Kentsu started out early as always. The summer sky was clear, the sun was warm and the hawks wheeled lazily in the sky.

"Buy some wine, some very fine wine!" Kentsu called as he trudged through the villages along the shore of the sea. But on that particular day, something was wrong, for no one seemed to want any of his wine. Even when he reached the farthest village at the foot of the hills, his jars were as heavy as they had been when he set out.

Kentsu sat down in the shade of a large cedar tree, wearily lowered his jars and sighed a great long sigh.

"*Yare yare*," he groaned. "This is a terrible way

to earn a living. Surely there must be something better that I could do." And he closed his eyes, too tired to move a single muscle.

As he sat there, he suddenly heard a high, shrill shriek coming from the beach. "Ah-eeee! Ah-eeee!" It was not the cry of a human being, nor did it sound like a bird. Kentsu sat silently and listened again. "Ah-eeee! Ah-eeee!" It sounded like a monkey and it seemed to be crying for help.

"I am too tired to go help a monkey," Kentsu murmured, but the cries were so plaintive, he could sit still no longer. He lifted the heavy jars to his shoulders once more and started toward the beach. As he neared the sand, he saw a little monkey with its paw thrust in the cleft of a large boulder. It was jumping up and down, flicking its tail and shrieking at the top of its voice.

"Here, here, little friend," Kentsu called. "What is the matter with you?" And he hurried to have a look.

"Ah, no wonder you are crying," Kentsu said sympathetically, for he saw that a giant crab gripped the little monkey's paw in its claws and would not let go. The more the monkey pulled, the harder the crab gripped.

"Ah-eeee!" the monkey wailed, and great tears rolled down its cheeks.

"Let go!" Kentsu called to the crab. But the crab wasn't going to let go now. "Let go!" Kentsu shouted again. Finally, he seized a stick and struck the crab until it released the monkey's paw and skittered back into the water. The monkey whimpered softly and licked its wounded paw.

"I'll take care of you, little friend," Kentsu said gently, and lifting the monkey to his back, he placed it between the two jars of wine. Then he carried it up to the hills and used his own handkerchief to bandage its paw with fragrant herbs.

"There, that should feel better," Kentsu consoled.

The monkey looked at him gratefully, calling, "Chi-chi-chee, chi-chi-chee." Then with a quick flick of its tail, it disappeared into the woods.

Kentsu felt better, and even though he hadn't sold any of his wine, he went home with a light heart.

It was two or three days later that Kentsu saw the monkey again. He had just been to the last village on his route and was walking slowly through the wooded hills when the monkey swung down from one of the trees. Kentsu saw his handkerchief still bound around the monkey's paw and he called out, "Well, little friend, how is your paw today?"

The monkey chattered urgently as though it had something important to tell him. "What is it?" Kentsu asked. "What are you trying to say?"

The monkey continued to chatter and finally began to tug at Kentsu's clothes.

"Here, here, stop it," Kentsu protested. "These are the only trousers I have. If you tear these, I won't be able to go out to sell my wine."

Still the monkey would not stop tugging, and at last Kentsu realized that it wanted to take him somewhere.

"So you want to show me something, do you?" he asked. "All right, I'll come with you." And he followed the monkey up into the hills.

The monkey clambered along over the narrow mountain path, going higher and higher. Soon the trees were so thick Kentsu could scarcely see the sky, and the sun disappeared behind masses of shadowy leaves. There was no path in the tall, thick grass and Kentsu stumbled over fallen branches and roots. Still the monkey went on and on. Kentsu had never gone so far up into the hills before. Suppose there were ogres or evil spirits lurking in the dark shadows! Hearing the ghostly rustle of the wind in the trees, Kentsu shivered.

"Little friend, I think I will stop and turn back now," he said fearfully. Perhaps the monkey itself was an evil spirit luring him to danger.

But the monkey came once more to tug at his trousers and would not let him turn back. It led Kentsu on and on, until finally they came to a cluster of moss-covered rocks. Then, at last, the monkey stopped beside some blue flowers that looked like a patch of sky fallen on the forest floor. Kentsu looked around and saw that behind the flowers and rocks there was a deep mountain pool so still and clear he could almost see himself in it. Kentsu sat down beside the monkey and sighed wearily.

"Ah-ah, so you brought me all the way up here just to show me a mountain pool," he murmured. "Why, I could have had a cool drink of water down in the village."

But the monkey chattered noisily and continued to pull Kentsu toward the pool until at last Kentsu bent down to scoop up some of the cool water. As he did, he sniffed. "That's strange," he said. "This water smells exactly like wine. I suppose it must be because I carry so much wine on my shoulders all day!"

Then he took a sip of the water. First just a little, and then more, and still more. He smacked his lips, shook his head in wonderment and tasted some more.

"Why, this is wine!" he shouted to the monkey. "The pool is all wine! It isn't water at all. It's a mountain pool of wine and I believe you knew it all along!"

He raised the monkey to his shoulders and danced around the pool shouting, "A never-ending pool of wine!" This was the most wonderful thing he had ever seen in his whole life, and the wine was better than the very best wine he had ever tasted.

"Just think," he said to the little monkey, "you led me all this way to show me this wonderful secret mountain pool."

Kentsu bowed to the monkey. "You are the finest monkey that ever lived. I would save you from a hundred crabs for what you have done for me," he declared, "and I thank you a thousand times over."

Now he would no longer have to buy wine from the village wine merchant, for here was a never-ending supply of wine and it was all free. Kentsu hurried down the mountain, talking and singing all the way, and when he had thanked the monkey once more at the foot of the mountain, he ran home to his village.

"Chi-chi-cheee," the monkey called one last time in farewell, and then it disappeared into the shadows of the forest.

From the very next day, Kentsu followed a different route. Instead of going to his own village first, he took his empty jars and went straight to the mountain pool. There he filled his jars with the sweet mountain wine and then starting at the farthest village, he gradually came back to his own.

Since the wine was free, Kentsu sold it at half the price he had charged before, and now everyone flocked eagerly to buy his wine, for it not only tasted better, it was cheaper as well. Kentsu still sang his same chant, but the wine sold so quickly, he scarcely had any left by the time he returned to his own village.

One day all of Kentsu's wine was sold at noon and there was still a half day left. "If I fill my jars once more," he thought, "I could sell twice as much wine and make twice as much money." It seemed a fine idea and now, at last, perhaps he could become a wealthy man.

He picked up his empty jars and rushed to the mountain pool puffing breathlessly in his hurry. But when he reached the pool and bent down to fill his jars, he discovered that the pool was as empty and dry as an old wooden keg.

"That's strange," Kentsu thought. "It was bubbling with wine just this morning. Surely it cannot have gone dry in half a day."

Kentsu sat down to ponder this strange happening. He knew no one else had discovered the pool, but it was indeed dry and empty. He went home puzzled and worried and could scarcely wait until the next morning to see if it would be full again. He was up at dawn and rushed once more to the mountainside. When he reached the pool, it was bubbling with wine just as before. Now, at last, Kentsu understood.

"Ah, I see," he said to himself. "The pool gives me enough to fill my jars just once a day so I can continue to sell wine as I have done all these years. I was not meant to sell twice as much wine and make twice as much money to become a wealthy man."

Kentsu went slowly down the hill, feeling ashamed of himself for having had such greedy thoughts. "I will never be so greedy again," he vowed.

And from that day, Kentsu even changed the words of his chant as he went from village to village selling his wine.

"Buy some wine, some very fine wine," he called. "One drink is just enough, two is just a little too much, and three is more than is good for you!"

"What's this?" the villagers asked. "Are you no longer anxious to sell your wine?"

But Kentsu simply answered, "One mustn't want too much of a good thing, for enough of something is just enough."

Although the people didn't quite understand what Kentsu meant, they bought more of his wine than ever before, and he never came home with a jar of unsold wine.

Kentsu did not become a wealthy man, but he was never poor again. The people of the village always said of him, "There goes a man who is happy and content." And Kentsu never asked for more than that.

THE TENGU'S MAGIC NOSE FAN

There once lived a good-for-nothing, do-nothing young man named Kotaro, who did nothing all day but play with a pair of dice. Instead of working like the other young men of the village, he would lure his friends away from work saying, "Come along with me, gambling is much more fun than working!" If he could find no one to play with, he would sit by himself, rattle his dice and try to think of some clever trick he might play on some unsuspecting villager.

One day when he could think of nothing wicked to do in the village, Kotaro went for a walk in the woods. When the sun grew hot, he sat in the shade of a tree and took out his dice. As he sat there shaking them and tossing them on the ground, he suddenly heard a rustling behind him. Kotaro turned quickly, and there peering over his shoulder was a large red nose. Behind the nose was the biggest long-nosed goblin he had ever seen in his whole life.

"H-h-h-help! It's a *tengu*!" Kotaro shouted and he leaped to his feet to run away.

But the *tengu* held him fast by the back of the neck. "Ho! Wait a moment," he said in a hoary voice. "Tell me what it is that you play with."

"Y-y-y-yes, sir," Kotaro stammered. "These—these are—d-d-d-dice. If you carry them with you always, you are bound to win some money someday."

The *tengu* reached out a hairy red arm and took the dice from Kotaro. He rattled them in his hand and grinned. "Hmmm," he said, "they make a pleasant sound."

Suddenly, the *tengu* thrust a big round fan in front of Kotaro. "I'll trade with you," he said. "I shall give you my fan if you give me your dice."

Kotaro hesitated. He was very fond of his dice, and what would he ever do with a battered old fan.

But the *tengu* went on. "This is not an ordinary fan, you know. It is a special magic nose fan."

"A nose fan?" Kotaro asked, puzzled. "Is it to cool your nose?"

The *tengu* laughed a big red horny laugh. "No,

stupid fellow," he said. "Fan it with one side and your nose will grow. Fan it with the other side and your nose will shrink. It's that kind of nose fan."

Kotaro laughed just thinking of the fun he could have with such a magic fan. "All right, I'll trade with you," he said eagerly, and he hurried home carrying his new nose fan instead of his dice.

The very next morning, he left home early wondering what mischief he could do with his new fan. As he walked along, he found himself in front of the mansion of the wealthiest man of the village. In a few moments the beautiful daughter of the house came strolling out through the gate.

"Ah, now for some fun!" Kotaro thought.

He hurried toward the young girl, and as he brushed past, he waved his fan in front of her face. Flap, flap—flap, flap. Then he ran away.

Suddenly the young girl screamed. "My nose! Something has happened to my nose!" she shrieked, as she ran back into the house. And indeed something had happened to her nose. It grew and it grew and it grew, until at last it was a foot long. The poor young girl shut herself in her room and hid under the quilts, weeping until she had no more tears.

"Summon all the doctors of the county," her father commanded, and soon the house was filled with doctors of all sizes and shapes. There were big doctors and small doctors, fat doctors and skinny doctors.

"Hmmm, a very strange case," they said, shaking their heads, but not one of them could make the girl's nose small again.

"Summon more doctors from all of Japan," her father commanded, and soon there were more doctors than ever swarming about the big mansion. But not one of them could fix the poor girl's nose. They rummaged about in their small black bags and sighed, "Alas, alas, we have no medicine at all to make a long nose short."

Finally, the father posted a sign in the village square that read, "Anyone who can help my daughter will have her hand in marriage and become heir to all my wealth."

Kotaro saw the sign and nodded his head. "Now is my chance!" he said to himself.

Carrying his fan in a small black bag, he hurried to the house of the wealthy man.

"I believe I can cure your daughter," he said, trying to look solemn and wise.

"Ah, you have some new medicine?" the father asked anxiously.

Kotaro shook his head mysteriously. "I have no medicine, but I have special magic powers with which I can cure her," he answered.

The father led him at once to his daughter's room. "Sir," he said, "if you can help my child, I shall give you anything. My daughter, my house, my money—they are all yours."

Kotaro acted as though he were the greatest doctor in all the land. "Clear the room," he commanded haughtily. Then when the doctors and servants were gone, he sat down beside the young girl and examined her nose.

"Hmmm," he murmured. Then, "Hmmm," once more. "A very strange case!" He told the girl to close her eyes, and quickly he took out his *tengu* fan and flapped it several times in front of her nose. Flap, flap. Her nose grew shorter. Flap, flap—flap, flap. Her nose grew shorter still. He continued to flap until at last her nose was exactly the size it should be. Then he put his fan back in his bag and told the girl to open her eyes.

"There you are," he said arrogantly. "I believe I have cured your nose."

When the father came in and saw what Kotaro had accomplished, he showered him with words of praise. "You have done what no doctor could do," he said gratefully. "Now to keep my promise, I shall give you my daughter for your wife and name you heir to all my wealth."

From that moment, Kotaro was treated as one of the family. He was given a beautiful room that looked out on the garden of moss and stone. He was given robes of silk and brocade, and a purse filled with golden coins. And then he was served the most delicious and magnificent meal the servants could prepare. Nothing was too good for Kotaro in the home of the wealthiest man of the village.

"I have done quite well for myself with this fan," Kotaro said to himself. "The people in this house are all fools."

With all the excitement, he grew hot and tired, and he stepped out into the garden to cool himself. "I'll just close my eyes and rest for a while," he thought, and stretching out on the moss, he began to fan himself. He fanned and dozed, fanned and dozed, and he did not remember that the fan in his hand was the very magic nose fan he had just used on the young girl. As he fanned himself, his nose began to grow. It grew and it grew and it grew and it grew. It soared straight up into the sky, growing longer and longer until it grew right through the floor of heaven.

Now at that very moment, the people of heaven were trying to build a bridge across the Milky Way. "Just one more piling," they said, looking about, "and our bridge will be finished."

As they looked about for a good-sized log, up through the clouds came Kotaro's long nose. "Ah, this is exactly what we need," said the people of heaven. "It is a little skinny, but it will do." And quickly they bound Kotaro's nose fast to their heavenly bridge.

It was then that Kotaro woke up. "Ouch!" he cried. "What's happened to my nose?" But by then, it was too late. Kotaro's nose had already become a permanent piling in the heavenly bridge.

"Help, help!" Kotaro shouted. Quickly, he turned his fan over and fanned as hard as he could. "Hurry, hurry! Grow short, grow short!" he shouted as he fanned.

Slowly his nose began to grow shorter, but as it was tied securely to the bridge in heaven, Kotaro's body had to fly upward to meet the end of his nose.

Up and up he flew, but halfway there he dropped his fan and he could not quite reach the end of his nose. There he stopped, dangling between heaven and earth.

"Help! Save me! Somebody, do something!" he cried.

Kotaro shouted and called until he was hoarse, but of course no one heard him or saw him, and no one at all could help him no matter how much he fussed and fumed.

It is quite possible, in fact, that he is there still, for no one in his village ever missed him or his mischievous tricks, and who knows, perhaps he may just dangle there forever.

THE MAGIC PURSE OF THE SWAMP MAIDEN

Long ago in a small village of Japan, there lived a young farmer who was very, very poor. In the spring of the year, the people of his village planned a pilgrimage to the great shrine at Ise, and for weeks ahead, there was talk of nothing else.

More than anything, the young farmer wanted to go with the pilgrims. He thought of the journey day and night but there was nothing he could do. He had scarcely enough money to feed and clothe himself, and it was useless for him even to dream of going.

As he heard his friends making plans for the trip, he grew more and more desolate.

At last the day of departure arrived, and early in the morning when the mist still stretched hazily over the rice fields, a group of villagers set out for the Ise Shrine. They carried baskets of food and bundles of clothing and started out with much singing and talking and laughter. The poor farmer watched sadly, as growing smaller and smaller, they disappeared down the dusty road.

"*Sayonara*! Keep well!" he called, and he was filled with longing to go with them.

As he walked back through the village to his small farm, he realized that at least one person from every house in the village had gone on the pilgrimage. By the time he got home, he could no longer bear the thought of staying behind. Before he quite knew what he was doing, he wrapped some rice cakes and clothing in a *furoshiki* and hurried down the road the villagers had taken.

"If I can just get to the shrine somehow, surely the gods will help me find a way to return," the farmer said to himself. Singing with happiness at the thought of being able to worship at the Ise Shrine with his friends and holding his head high, he walked quickly down the winding road. He watched carefully for those who had gone ahead, but no matter how far he went, the road remained empty and deserted.

"That's strange," the farmer thought. "I must have taken a wrong turn somewhere, for I surely should have overtaken them by now."

He paused a moment at the crest of a hill and looked down at the road that stretched out before him. It was a road he had not seen before, and it seemed to lead straight to the terrible Black Swamp that everyone feared.

"I don't want to go near that terrible swamp," the farmer thought. Although he looked in every direction, there was no other road for him to take.

"Perhaps this is a short cut the townspeople have taken, and I will see them soon," he told himself, and slowly he went down the hill and edged his way toward the Black Swamp.

As he drew closer, the sky became a smoldering mass of black thunder clouds, a shrill wind began to howl and torrents of rain lashed around his head. The farmer shuddered and drew his straw cape tight around his shoulders, but he plodded on, thinking he could overtake his friends if they stopped for shelter.

As he trudged along beside the murky waters of the swamp, he heard someone call to him.

"Ah, someone has found me at last," he thought happily. But when he turned, he saw a strange young girl walking toward him from the middle of the swamp. Her hair hung long and black, and her silvery blue

dress shimmered faintly in the dusky light. Although she walked through the waters of the swamp, she was neither muddy nor wet, and a mysterious, lonely smile hovered over her lips.

"Don't be afraid, my friend," she called, as the farmer stepped back. "It was I who called you and it was I who made you take the wrong turn and miss your friends. You are a good and kind man," she added. "Won't you help me?"

"I—I— will if I can," the farmer stammered, wondering what this lovely creature of the swamp could want of a poor farmer like him.

"You have heard of the Red Swamp near Osaka?" she asked, coming a little closer.

The farmer shuddered just to hear the name. "Of course," he said. "No one ever comes out of that swamp alive, for it is even more terrible than this swamp."

"My mother and father live in the Red Swamp," the girl explained calmly, "and all I ask is that you take a letter to them so they will know I am well."

The farmer backed away in alarm. "Your parents live in the Red Swamp?" he asked cautiously. He knew that if he went there, he might never get to Ise at all.

In fact, he would probably never get out alive or ever return to his village.

"I'm sorry, but I just can't do that," he began.

As he spoke, great tears rolled down the young girl's cheeks.

"The Ruler of the Black Swamp will never let me leave, and I can never see my parents again," she sobbed. "Please, just take this letter to them so they will know I think of them."

The gentle farmer felt so sorry for the young girl, he could no longer refuse. "Very well then," he said, and he agreed at last to take the long white envelope that she held out to him. As soon as he had, she pressed upon him a small red purse that bulged with golden coins.

"This is a magic purse," she explained. "Spend as much as you like, but always leave one coin in it and by the next morning the purse will be full once more. Use the money for your travels," she said, "and my thanks go with you always, good friend."

The farmer started to speak, but already the beautiful young girl had disappeared into the darkness of the swamp. As the farmer looked all around, he saw only a gentle mist rising from the waters. And from somewhere in the distance, he heard a plaintive voice calling, "Don't forget me—don't forget me—don't forget—" Then it died away like an echo and there was only the singing of a lonely cricket in the stillness.

The farmer shivered, and when he looked up, he saw that the clouds were gone and the sun was out once more to warm the land.

"I must have dreamed the whole thing," the farmer muttered, but the red purse in his hand was very real and it was still heavy with the coins of gold. He shook his head, wondering at the whole strange adventure, and then hurried on toward the Red Swamp. He had promised the young girl and he had her letter. Now he must go whether he wanted to or not.

The farmer traveled on, and as he neared Osaka, he stopped to ask the way to the Red Swamp. Each person he asked was horrified. "The Red Swamp! Why do you want to go there?" they cried. "You will never come out alive."

Several times the farmer thought of throwing away the letter and going on to Ise, but he remembered the tears of the strange young girl. He could still hear her thin, high voice calling, "Don't forget—don't forget—" and he knew he could not break his promise to her.

At last he came to the edge of the terrible Red Swamp. It was surrounded with giant gnarled trees heavy with streamers of moss, and its steamy waters churned with slithering snakes. The farmer shuddered and forced himself to walk on. There was no one for miles around, and he knew that even if he were to call for help, no one would hear him. He proceeded warily, watching carefully for danger on all sides.

When he decided he had gone far enough, the farmer stopped and clapped his hands to announce his arrival. The sound echoed hollowly through the lonely swamp, but nothing seemed to stir. The farmer clapped once more, and then slowly the waters of the swamp began to churn and an old man with a white beard appeared before him in a small boat.

"Ah, you have come with the letter," he said, as though he knew exactly why the farmer had come.

"Yes, yes," the farmer answered. "I have brought word from your daughter to tell you she is well."

The old man bowed. "I am ever grateful," he said. "And now, please step into the boat and come with me."

The farmer was anxious to give him the letter and hurry away from the swamp. "I have come only to give you the letter," he said, backing away. "I must be on my way."

The old man smiled. "Do not be frightened, my friend," he said. "I know the swamp well and I promise to return you to this spot unharmed."

The farmer swallowed hard. Suppose the boat sank into the blackness of the swamp and disappeared forever. No one would ever find him, and no one would know what became of him. But now the old man reached out to help him into the boat.

"Come," he urged. "Please come. I promise that you will be safe."

"Well then," the farmer said, and as soon as he stepped into the boat, a wave of sleepiness overwhelmed him. He tried hard to keep his eyes open, but they felt as though they were weighted with stones. The farmer finally fell asleep and when he awoke, he found himself in a beautiful room with the old man and his wife sitting before him.

"You were very kind to bring us this letter from our daughter," they said. "We can't tell you how happy you have made us." And they wept with joy as they read the long letter from their daughter in the Black Swamp.

Soon the old woman brought out golden lacquer trays laden with such food as the farmer had never seen in his life. There were lobster and sea bream, fish roe and quail's eggs. There were fried bumblebees and turtle chowder and squid and black mushrooms. The farmer ate until he could eat no more. Then the old woman spread out several soft silken quilts for him, and the farmer soon fell sound asleep.

When he awoke early the next morning, the farmer found another golden tray beside his pillow. This one, however, was not laden with food. Instead, it was heaped high with coins of gold.

"They are for you. You must take them," the old man and woman insisted. "It is the only way we can thank you for the great kindness you have done."

Now the farmer had not only his magic purse but another bag filled with the gold coins from the tray. "You have been very kind," he said to the old people, "but now I must be on my way."

He climbed once more into the little boat, blinked once, and in an instant the old man had brought him to the edge of the swamp where they had first met.

"Thank you, old man," the farmer said bowing. "I shall never forget you."

When he looked up, the old man was gone. Again, it all seemed like a dream, but the bag he held in his hand was indeed real and heavy with gold.

The farmer ran out into the spring sunshine shouting, "I have been in the terrible Red Swamp and I am safe and well!"

He had not been swallowed up by a dragon or a crocodile nor had he stepped into any quicksand or whirlpools. Besides that, he was now so rich he could travel to Ise in great comfort. He hurried to the shrine with a heart full of happiness and a purse full of gold. When he arrived, however, he found that his friends had already come and gone. He worshipped alone at the shrine and thanked the gods for his good fortune.

"How fortunate that I started out on this pilgrimage after all," he thought. Then he hurried back to his village.

"What happened to you?" the villagers asked when he came home at last. "Where have you been and what have you been doing?"

Quickly the farmer told them about the lonely maiden of the Black Swamp and of the letter he had taken to her parents in the Red Swamp. "And look," he added, showing them his magic purse and the gold coins in his bag. "For the first time in all my life, I am no longer poor!"

"Only a very brave man would have ventured alone into the Red Swamp," the villagers said with admiration. "And only a very kind man would have carried the letter there as he had promised," they added.

Everyone agreed that the farmer surely deserved the wealth he now had, and they rejoiced with him.

The farmer built a new house and he bought cows and horses and pigs, and he hired many people to work for him. He helped his friends, and he never failed to give money to the poor or to anyone who was in need. Even so, he remained the wealthiest man of the village, for whenever his purse was almost empty, he had only to leave one coin in it and by next morning, it was always full.

The farmer never forgot the beautiful young girl in the swamp who had brought him such good fortune. Each year, when the cherry trees became clouds of white along the riverbanks, he took a tray of rice cakes and wine to the Black Swamp and let it float away on the water. The next day when he returned, the tray drifted back empty, so he knew that the young girl had received his gifts. She never appeared to the farmer again, but even after many years, he could hear her gentle voice calling, "Don't forget me—don't forget me—don't forget me—" And for all his remaining days, he never did.

THE TWO FOOLISH CATS

Once in a long ago time, there were two cats who lived together in the hills of Japan. One was a very large black cat and the other was a small tabby about half his size. They were the best of friends, and never said an unkind word to each other until one day when each of them found a wonderfully fresh rice cake.

"Look what I have found!" the big cat called, holding his rice cake gently in his paws. He sniffed its sweet smell and purred with contentment. "Is this not the most delicious-looking rice cake you have ever seen?" he asked.

But the small cat held up his own rice cake, saying, "Yes, but just look at mine. It looks even more delicious than a plump field mouse!"

The two cats sat down under a tree at the side of the road to compare their rice cakes. As each held up his cake to show the other, they discovered that the big cat's rice cake was quite small and the little cat's rice cake a great deal larger.

"That's not fair at all," the big cat pouted. "I am bigger, so naturally I should have the bigger rice cake. Here, let us trade."

But the little cat growled and showed his teeth. "That's not so," he cried. "Because I am small I need more food so I can grow. I shall never, never trade with you."

"Eoowrrr, you are very fresh for a small cat!"

"Eoowrrr, you are very greedy for a big cat!"

The two cats scowled and snarled and spit and soon began to chase each other around the trees. They clawed and scratched. They spit and scowled. They hissed and yowled for hours and hours, but neither one would give in. At last the big black cat stopped to catch his breath.

"This will never do," he said. "We might be fighting for another week like this. Let us go to see the wise monkey of the forest and have him divide our rice cakes equally. Then each of us will have a fair share."

"Very well," the small cat agreed, for he wanted to stop fighting over the rice cakes and put one in his mouth. If they did not stop quarreling soon, the rice cakes would grow hard and stale.

So the two cats hurried into the woods to look for the wise monkey who lived in the treetops. They scampered along curving paths that wound around the trees, and they clambered over logs and crept through the tall grasses and vines as they searched for the monkey.

"Mr. Monkey, Mr. Monkey," the big cat called. "We need you to settle a quarrel for us."

At last they found the wise old monkey, with a red hat and a pair of golden scales, sitting on the branch of a tree. He looked as though he could solve all the problems of the world.

The two cats held out their rice cakes and in high, squeaky voices began to chatter all at once.

"One at a time. Please, one at a time," the monkey scolded. And when each cat had stated his case, the monkey nodded slowly.

"Aha, I see," he said, looking very wise and solemn. "You were right to come to me with your problem, for I shall see that you each receive an equal share, and I shall put an end to your quarreling."

The cats nodded knowingly. They had been

sensible indeed to bring their problem to the monkey.

Now the monkey turned to his golden scales and put one rice cake on each side. Of course the scales did not balance, for the big rice cake was heavier.

"You were quite right to quarrel," the monkey said, pointing to the scales. "You see, one rice cake is quite a bit heavier than the other." He quickly took the larger rice cake and took a bite out of it. "Now," he said, "that should make them both equal."

But the monkey had taken too big a bite, for now the smaller rice cake was heavier. "Oh, this will never do," he wailed, and this time he took a bite from the smaller rice cake.

When he put it back on the scales, it was plain to see that again he had taken too much. Once more he took a bite from the other rice cake to make the scales balance.

"Ahem," the big cat said, squirming uncomfortably. "I believe you have taken enough, sir."

"Yes, yes, surely they must be equal by now," the little cat added timidly.

But the clever old monkey did not pay the slightest bit of attention to either of them. He went

right on weighing and munching, weighing and munching, until at last he had eaten up both rice cakes completely and the scales were empty.

Then he looked at the two cats. "Well, well, they are now both equally gone," he said with a sly look. "I promised I would end your quarreling and indeed I have, for now there is nothing more for you to quarrel about." And with a quick flick of his tail, the monkey disappeared into the woods.

"Eoowrrr, I feel stupidly foolish," the big cat said dismally.

"Eoowrrr, I feel foolishly stupid," the little cat added.

The two cats went slinking down the road, empty-handed and hungry, and from that day on, they never quarreled again.

THE WISE OLD WOMAN

Many long years ago, there lived an arrogant and cruel young lord who ruled over a small village in the western hills of Japan.

"I have no use for old people in my village," he said haughtily. "They are neither useful nor able to work for a living. I therefore decree that anyone over seventy-one must be banished from the village and left in the mountains to die."

"What a dreadful decree! What a cruel and unreasonable lord we have," the people of the village murmured. But the lord fearfully punished anyone who disobeyed him, and so villagers who turned seventy-one were tearfully carried into the mountains, never to return.

Gradually there were fewer and fewer old people in the village and soon they disappeared altogether. Then the young lord was pleased.

"What a fine village of young, healthy and hard-working people I have," he bragged. "Soon it will be the finest village in all of Japan."

Now there lived in this village a kind young farmer and his aged mother. They were poor, but the farmer was good to his mother, and the two of them lived happily together. However, as the years went by, the mother grew older, and before long she reached the terrible age of seventy-one.

"If only I could somehow deceive the cruel lord," the farmer thought. But there were records in the village books and every one knew that his mother had turned seventy-one.

Each day the son put off telling his mother that he must take her into the mountains to die, but the people of the village began to talk. The farmer knew that if he did not take his mother away soon, the lord would send his soldiers and throw them both into a dark dungeon to die a terrible death.

"Mother—" he would begin, as he tried to tell her what he must do, but he could not go on.

Then one day the mother herself spoke of the lord's dread decree. "Well, my son," she said, "the time has come for you to take me to the mountains.

We must hurry before the lord sends his soldiers for you." And she did not seem worried at all that she must go to the mountains to die.

"Forgive me, dear mother, for what I must do," the farmer said sadly, and the next morning he lifted his mother to his shoulders and set off on the steep path toward the mountains. Up and up he climbed, until the trees clustered close and the path was gone. There was no longer even the sound of birds, and they heard only the soft wail of the wind in the trees. The son walked slowly, for he could not bear to think of leaving his old mother in the mountains. On and on he climbed, not wanting to stop and leave her behind. Soon, he heard his mother breaking off small twigs from the trees that they passed.

"Mother, what are you doing?" he asked.

"Do not worry, my son," she answered gently. "I am just marking the way so you will not get lost returning to the village."

The son stopped. "Even now you are thinking of me?" he asked, wonderingly.

The mother nodded. "Of course, my son," she replied. "You will always be in my thoughts. How could it be otherwise?"

At that, the young farmer could bear it no longer. "Mother, I cannot leave you in the mountains to die all alone," he said. "We are going home and no matter what the lord does to punish me, I will never desert you again."

So they waited until the sun had set and a lone star crept into the silent sky. Then in the dark shadows of night, the farmer carried his mother down the hill and they returned quietly to their little house. The farmer dug a deep hole in the floor of his kitchen and made a small room where he could hide his mother. From that day, she spent all her time in the secret room and the farmer carried meals to her there. The rest of the time, he was careful to work in the fields and act as though he lived alone. In this way, for almost two years, he kept his mother safely hidden and no one in the village knew that she was there.

Then one day there was a terrible commotion among the villagers for Lord Higa of the town beyond the hills threatened to conquer their village and make it his own.

"Only one thing can spare you," Lord Higa announced. "Bring me a box containing one thousand ropes of ash and I will spare your village."

The cruel young lord quickly gathered together all the wise men of his village. "You are men of wisdom," he said. "Surely you can tell me how to meet Lord Higa's demands so our village can be spared."

But the wise men shook their heads. "It is impossible to make even one rope of ash, sire," they answered. "How can we ever make one thousand?"

"Fools!" the lord cried angrily. "What good is your wisdom if you cannot help me now?"

And he posted a notice in the village square offering a great reward of gold to any villager who could help him save their village.

But all the people in the village whispered, "Surely, it is an impossible thing, for ash crumbles at the touch of the finger. How could anyone ever make a rope of ash?" They shook their heads and sighed, "Alas, alas, we must be conquered by yet another cruel lord."

The young farmer, too, supposed that this must be, and he wondered what would happen to his mother if a new lord even more terrible than their own came to rule over them.

When his mother saw the troubled look on his face, she asked, "Why are you so worried, my son?"

So the farmer told her of the impossible demand

made by Lord Higa if the village was to be spared, but his mother did not seem troubled at all. Instead she laughed softly and said, "Why, that is not such an impossible task. All one has to do is soak ordinary rope in salt water and dry it well. When it is burned, it will hold its shape and there is your rope of ash! Tell the villagers to hurry and find one thousand pieces of rope."

The farmer shook his head in amazement. "Mother, you are wonderfully wise," he said, and he rushed to tell the young lord what he must do.

"You are wiser than all the wise men of the village," the lord said when he heard the farmer's solution, and he rewarded him with many pieces of gold. The thousand ropes of ash were quickly made and the village was spared.

In a few days, however, there was another great commotion in the village as Lord Higa sent another threat. This time he sent a log with a small hole that curved and bent seven times through its length, and he demanded that a single piece of silk thread be threaded through the hole. "If you cannot perform this task," the lord threatened, "I shall come to conquer your village."

The young lord hurried once more to his wise men, but they all shook their heads in bewilderment. "A needle cannot bend its way through such curves," they moaned. "Again we are faced with an impossible demand."

"And again you are stupid fools!" the lord said, stamping his foot impatiently. He then posted a second notice in the village square asking the villagers for their help.

Once more the young farmer hurried with the problem to his mother in her secret room.

"Why, that is not so difficult," his mother said with a quick smile. "Put some sugar at one end of the hole. Then, tie an ant to a piece of silk thread and put it in at the other end. He will weave his way in and out of the curves to get to the sugar and he will take the silk thread with him."

"Mother, you are remarkable!" the son cried, and he hurried off to the lord with the solution to the second problem.

Once more the lord commended the young farmer and rewarded him with many pieces of gold. "You are a brilliant man and you have saved our village again," he said gratefully.

But the lord's troubles were not over even then, for a few days later Lord Higa sent still another demand. "This time you will undoubtedly fail and then I shall conquer your village," he threatened. "Bring me a drum that sounds without being beaten."

"But that is not possible," sighed the people of the village. "How can anyone make a drum sound without beating it?"

This time the wise men held their heads in their hands and moaned, "It is hopeless. It is hopeless. This time Lord Higa will conquer us all."

The young farmer hurried home breathlessly. "Mother, Mother, we must solve another terrible problem or Lord Higa will conquer our village!" And he quickly told his mother about the impossible drum.

His mother, however, smiled and answered, "Why, this is the easiest of them all. Make a drum with sides of paper and put a bumblebee inside. As it tries to escape, it will buzz and beat itself against the paper and you will have a drum that sounds without being beaten."

The young farmer was amazed at his mother's wisdom. "You are far wiser than any of the wise men of the village," he said, and he hurried to tell the

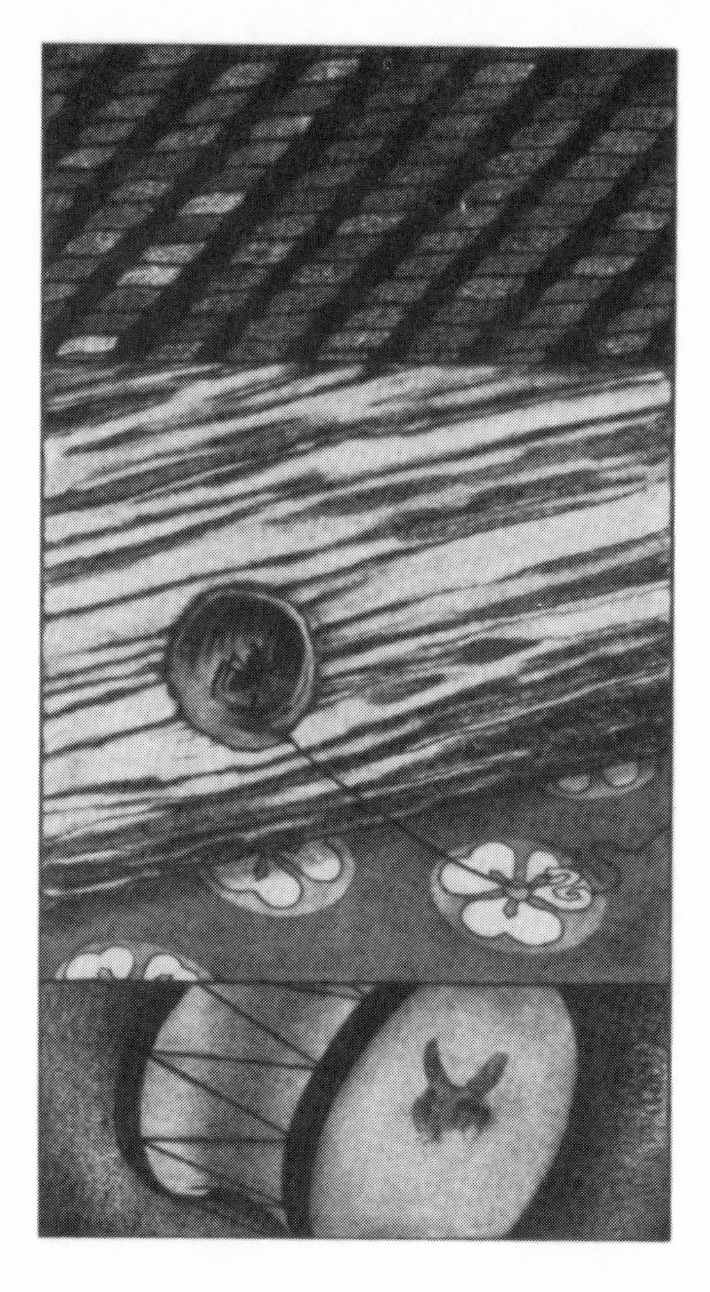

young lord how to meet Lord Higa's third demand.

When the lord heard the answer, he was greatly impressed. "Surely a young man like you cannot be wiser than all my wise men," he said. "Tell me honestly, who has helped you solve all these difficult problems?"

The young farmer could not lie. "My lord," he began slowly, "for the past two years I have broken the law of the land. I have kept my aged mother hidden beneath the floor of my house, and it is she who solved each of your problems and saved the village from Lord Higa."

He trembled as he spoke, for he feared the lord's displeasure and rage. Surely now the soldiers would be summoned to throw him into the dark dungeon. But when he glanced fearfully at the lord, he saw that the young ruler was not angry at all. Instead, he was silent and thoughtful, for at last he realized how much wisdom and knowledge old people possess.

"I have been very wrong," he said finally. "And I must ask the forgiveness of your mother and of all my people. Never again will I demand that the old people of our village be sent to the mountains to die. Rather, they will be treated with the respect and honor they deserve and share with us the wisdom of their years."

And so it was. From that day, the villagers were no longer forced to abandon their parents in the mountains, and the village became once more a happy, cheerful place in which to live. The terrible Lord Higa stopped sending his impossible demands and no longer threatened to conquer them, for he too was impressed. "Even in such a small village there is much wisdom," he declared, "and its people should be allowed to live in peace."

And that is exactly what the farmer and his mother and all the people of the village did for all the years thereafter.

THE OGRE WHO BUILT A BRIDGE

Long years ago, there was a small village that stood beside a swift and rumbling river. The river was so fierce and strong, in fact, that no one had ever been able to bridge it. Although many, many men had tried, not one could build a bridge that was strong enough to withstand the roaring waters of the great river.

"If only we had a bridge so we could cross to the village on the other bank," the villagers sighed. "Then we could trade with them and all of us would grow prosperous."

At last one day, they had a plan. "We will send for the best carpenter in all of Japan," they said. And they begged him to come saying, "You are the only one in all this country who can build us the bridge we need."

When the carpenter heard of their problem, he quickly agreed to come. "Of course I will help you," he said, "for I have built many bridges across many rivers, and I have no fear of your great river that will not be bridged."

As soon as the carpenter arrived in the village, he went to inspect the great and troublesome river. He gasped in surprise when he saw it for it was indeed a fearsome sight. He peered into its brown, murky waters, but it was so deep he could not see the bottom at all. And it was so wide, the opposite shore was only a faint, misty strip that seemed to float in the distant haze. The carpenter gazed silently at the rumbling water rushing over rocks and boulders, and it seemed to say, "Never, never, never will you build a bridge over me!"

The carpenter rubbed his forehead as a worrisome feeling swept over him. Of course he had built the best bridges in all of Japan, but never before over a river such as this. He could not give up now, however, for he had made a promise to the villagers and he must give them their bridge.

As the carpenter looked out at the churning water, he suddenly saw something enormous rise slowly to the surface from a mass of foaming bubbles. A giant head with two great horns gradually emerged from the river, spilling water as it rose like a thousand great waterfalls. The carpenter was knocked off his feet by a shower of water that filled the air as the giant head shook itself. Then, in a roaring voice, it called out, "*Oi!* Mr. Carpenter, why do you sit there looking troubled?"

The carpenter was so frightened, all he could do was quiver and shake. The great head that peered out at him from the river was the head of an enormous red ogre. On top of his head were two great horns, and his mouth was like a giant black cave that spread from ear to ear. The carpenter had never seen anything so frightening in all his life. He tried to speak, but all that came out was a tiny squeak.

"I— I— I—" he stammered.

"I know," the giant ogre shouted. "You want to build a bridge over this river. Isn't that so?"

The carpenter could only nod his head.

"But it is quite impossible for you to build a bridge across this wide and terrible river. Isn't that so?"

Again the carpenter nodded. "Y— Y— Yes, that is so," he answered, still trembling.

"So you are worried?"

"Yes, yes, that is true."

"Well, in that case, you can stop worrying, for I

will build the bridge for you. What is impossible for a puny human like you, is nothing for a great ogre like me," the ogre bragged. "Why, I could have the bridge built before breakfast tomorrow morning."

"Could you?" the carpenter asked. "Could you really?"

"An ogre never lies," the ogre said indignantly. "Of course I could. I will have the bridge built by morning."

The carpenter sighed happily to think that his problem was solved. "Well then," he said, "you must let me give you a gift in return for your help. Tell me, what could I give you?"

The ogre was silent for a moment. "Ah, a gift," he mused. "What useful thing could a puny human being give to a great ogre like me?"

He thought and he thought, turning his big horny head from side to side. Then, a slow grin spread over his face. "I have it," he shouted. "You may give me one of your eyeballs!"

The carpenter gasped. "My eyeball!" he objected. "But I have only two and they are very precious to me."

"But I am building you a bridge that no human

could ever build," the ogre answered coldly. "And besides, you have already promised me a gift."

The carpenter stood silent, not knowing what to say. He wanted the bridge very badly, but he did not want to give up even one of his precious eyeballs.

The ogre grinned once more and then said, "Since you are so troubled, I will give you one chance to save your eyeball. I will build your bridge anyway, and if by tomorrow morning you can tell me what my name is, I will let you keep your eyeball. Is that a bargain?"

The carpenter was sure he could somehow save himself by tomorrow. "I agree," he said in a small voice.

When he heard that, the giant ogre disappeared as suddenly as he had come. With a loud gurgle and a churning roar, he vanished into the depths of the river, leaving only a few bubbles to show he had been there at all.

All that long night the carpenter couldn't sleep as he worried and wondered about the ogre and the bridge. He fretted and tossed, and whenever he closed his eyes, he saw the ogre grinning at him and holding out his hand for the gift.

As the first faint light of morning streaked the sky the carpenter hurried to the river to see if the bridge was truly built. He half hoped it was, and he half hoped it wasn't. As he reached the pebbled beach along the river, he looked up, and there stood the most magnificent bridge he had ever seen. In the mist of early morning, it looked like a bridge to heaven. Its great curving arc swept over the frothing waters sturdy and strong, and yet it was as graceful as a willow tree. It was true. The ogre had built a bridge finer than any a human being could have built.

As the carpenter stood admiring the bridge, the waters of the river began to churn and boil, and from the frothing bubbles there emerged once more the enormous head of the red ogre.

"Well, Mr. Carpenter," he bellowed, "how do you like my bridge?"

"It is magnificent," the carpenter said dismally.

"Far better than any a human could have built?" the ogre asked.

The carpenter nodded.

"Well then," the ogre went on, "you must keep your promise and give me an eyeball."

"I have one more thing to ask of you," the carpenter said quickly. "Please give me just one more day to guess your name."

The ogre tossed his great red head and laughed until the ground under the carpenter seemed to crumble. "A puny human like you will never, never guess my name," he jeered. "But I will give you one more day and that is absolutely all." Then once more he disappeared into the water with a final, swishing roar.

The carpenter was so worried he didn't know what to do.

"I must think of something. I must save my eyeball! I must discover his name," he mumbled to himself. And hunched over with worry, he walked slowly toward the wooded hills behind the village. He had to think, and think very hard. He walked on and on, not realizing where he was going, and before long he was deep in the forest many, many miles from the little village by the river. The day was half gone and still he had no idea at all what the ogre's name might be.

"Ah me, what shall I do?" he moaned.

Then suddenly he heard the high, faint sound of a strange chant-like song. He stopped to listen, for it was not the singing of birds or beasts. It was the sound of children's voices.

"What could these children be doing so deep in the woods?" he wondered. "Perhaps they could tell me how to get back to the village."

The carpenter hurried toward the sound of the singing, but as he drew close, he saw that these were not ordinary children who danced and sang. On each small head there were two little horns and their mouths stretched in wide grins from ear to ear. These were small ogre children playing in the secret shadows of the forest. The carpenter felt a shiver run down his back. He must creep away quickly before they saw him. But as he turned to go, he heard the song they were singing.

"Mr. Ogre, Mr. Ogre, Mr. Ogre Roku,
Bring us the eyeball you got for the bridge!
Hurry up and come to us, Mr. Ogre Roku,
Bring us the eyeball you got for the bridge!"

They were singing about his eyeball! And they were singing about the red ogre of the river! Now, at last, he knew the ogre's name. He was saved! His eye was saved!

The carpenter scarcely dared breathe as he backed away, slowly, slowly, slowly, so he would not be seen. Then he ran pell-mell down the hill, stumbling and gasping and rushing until at last he found his way back to the village.

Early the next morning the carpenter hurried to the bridge, and as soon as he arrived, the great red head appeared from the water.

"Well, Mr. Carpenter," the ogre roared. "Are you ready to give me my gift?"

He rose slowly from the water and held out an enormous horny hand. But the carpenter shrank back.

"Just a minute, let me guess, let me guess," he said, for he did not want to give the answer too quickly and rouse the ogre's anger.

The ogre let out a watery, gurgling chuckle. "You will never guess, puny carpenter," he said scornfully.

The carpenter took a deep breath. "Is it Ogre of the Terrible River?"

"Ha, ha, ha—It is not!" roared the ogre.

"Is it Ogre of the Horny Head?"

"Ha, ha, ha—It is not! It is not!"

"Then, is it Giant Red Ogre?"

"You will never, never guess. Give me your eyeball, and give it to me now!"

Then the carpenter shouted in his loudest voice.

"I know, I know. It is Ogre Roku! That is your name. It is Ogre Roku! Ogre Roku!"

The great red ogre's mouth fell open in surprise as the grin disappeared from his face. "How did you know?" he shouted angrily.

Then without another word, the great red head suddenly vanished into the river depths with a tremendous swoosh. The bubbles churned and boiled and frothed and foamed, and then slowly, slowly, they faded away until all that was left was one giant bubble on top of the water.

"Ogre Roku!" the carpenter shouted once more for good measure. This time the single brown bubble popped and even that was gone. Then there was nothing to see but the busy waters of the river tumbling and rumbling and bumbling over the rocks and boulders. It was as though there never had been such a thing as the great red ogre at all. But when the carpenter looked up the river, the bridge still stood, forming a perfect arch over the rushing water.

"Ha, Red Ogre," the carpenter shouted, "thank you for the bridge!" Then he hurried back to tell the villagers what had happened.

"At last, you have a fine bridge to span the wild

river," he cried happily. "Never need you fear the terrible river again."

And so it was. The bridge was sturdy and firm, and it withstood the torrents of the mighty river. It brought prosperity to the villages on both sides of the river, and it brought fame and riches to the carpenter.

"We shall name the bridge after you," the villagers said gratefully to the carpenter.

But he shook his head. "Call it the Bridge of the Red Ogre," he said, and from that day on that is what the bridge was called.

NEW YEAR'S HATS FOR THE STATUES

Once a very kind old man and woman lived in a small house high in the hills of Japan. Although they were good people, they were very, very poor, for the old man made his living by weaving the reed hats that farmers used to ward off the sun and rain, and even in a year's time, he could not sell very many.

One cold winter day as the year was drawing to an end, the old woman said to the old man, "Good husband, it will soon be New Year's Day, but we have nothing in the house to eat. How will we welcome the new year without even a pot of fresh rice?" A worried frown hovered over her face, and she sighed sadly as she looked into her empty cupboards.

But the old man patted her shoulders and said, "Now, now, don't you worry. I will make some reed hats and take them to the village to sell. Then with the money I earn I will buy some fish and rice for our New Year's feast."

On the day before New Year's, the old man set out for the village with five new reed hats that he had made. It was bitterly cold, and from early morning, snow tumbled from the skies and blew in great drifts about their small house. The old man shivered in the wind, but he thought about the fresh warm rice and the fish turning crisp and brown over the charcoal, and he knew he must earn some money to buy them. He pulled his wool scarf tighter about his throat and plodded on slowly over the snow-covered roads.

When he got to the village, he trudged up and down its narrow streets calling, "Reed hats for sale! Reed hats for sale!" But everyone was too busy preparing for the new year to be bothered with reed hats. They scurried by him, going instead to the shops where they could buy sea bream and red beans and herring roe for their New Year's feasts. No one even bothered to look at the old man or his hats.

As the old man wandered about the village, the snow fell faster, and before long the sky began to grow dark. The old man knew it was useless to linger, and he sighed with longing as he passed the fish shop and saw the rows of fresh fish.

"If only I could bring home one small piece of

fish for my wife," he thought glumly, but his pockets were even emptier than his stomach.

There was nothing to do but to go home again with his five unsold hats. The old man headed wearily back toward his little house in the hills, bending his head against the biting cold of the wind. As he walked along, he came upon six stone statues of Jizo, the guardian god of children. They stood by the roadside covered with snow that had piled in small drifts on top of their heads and shoulders.

"*Mah, mah,* you are covered with snow," the old man said to the statues, and setting down his bundle, he stopped to brush the snow from their heads. As he was about to go on, a fine idea occurred to him.

"I am sorry these are only reed hats I could not sell," he apologized, "but at least they will keep the snow off your heads." And carefully he tied one on each of the Jizo statues.

"Now if I had one more there would be enough for each of them," he murmured as he looked at the row of statues. But the old man did not hesitate for long. Quickly he took the hat from his own head and tied it on the head of the sixth statue.

"There," he said looking pleased. "Now all of you are covered. Then, bowing in farewell, he told the statues that he must be going. "A happy new year to each of you," he called, and he hurried away content.

When he got home the old woman was waiting anxiously for him. "Did you sell your hats?" she asked. "Were you able to buy some rice and fish?"

The old man shook his head. "I couldn't sell a single hat," he explained, "but I did find a very good use for them." And he told her how he had put them on the Jizo statues that stood in the snow.

"Ah, that was a very kind thing to do," the old woman said. "I would have done exactly the same." And she did not complain at all that the old man had not brought home anything to eat. Instead she made some hot tea and added a precious piece of charcoal to the brazier so the old man could warm himself.

That night they went to bed early, for there was no more charcoal and the house had grown cold. Outside the wind continued to blow the snow in a white curtain that wrapped itself about the small house. The old man and woman huddled beneath their thick quilts and tried to keep warm.

"We are fortunate to have a roof over our heads on such a night," the old man said.

"Indeed we are," the old woman agreed, and before long they were both fast asleep.

About daybreak, when the sky was still a misty gray, the old man awakened for he heard voices outside.

"Listen," he whispered to the old woman.

"What is it? What is it?" the old woman asked.

Together they held their breath and listened. It sounded like a group of men pulling a very heavy load.

"*Yoi-sah! Hoi-sah! Yoi-sah! Hoi-sah!*" the voices called and seemed to come closer and closer.

"Who could it be so early in the morning?" the old man wondered. Soon, they heard the men singing.

Where is the home of the kind old man,
The man who covered our heads?
Where is the home of the kind old man,
Who gave us his hats for our heads?"

The old man and woman hurried to the window to look out, and there in the snow they saw the six stone Jizo statues lumbering toward their house. They still wore the reed hats the old man had given them and each one was pulling a heavy sack.

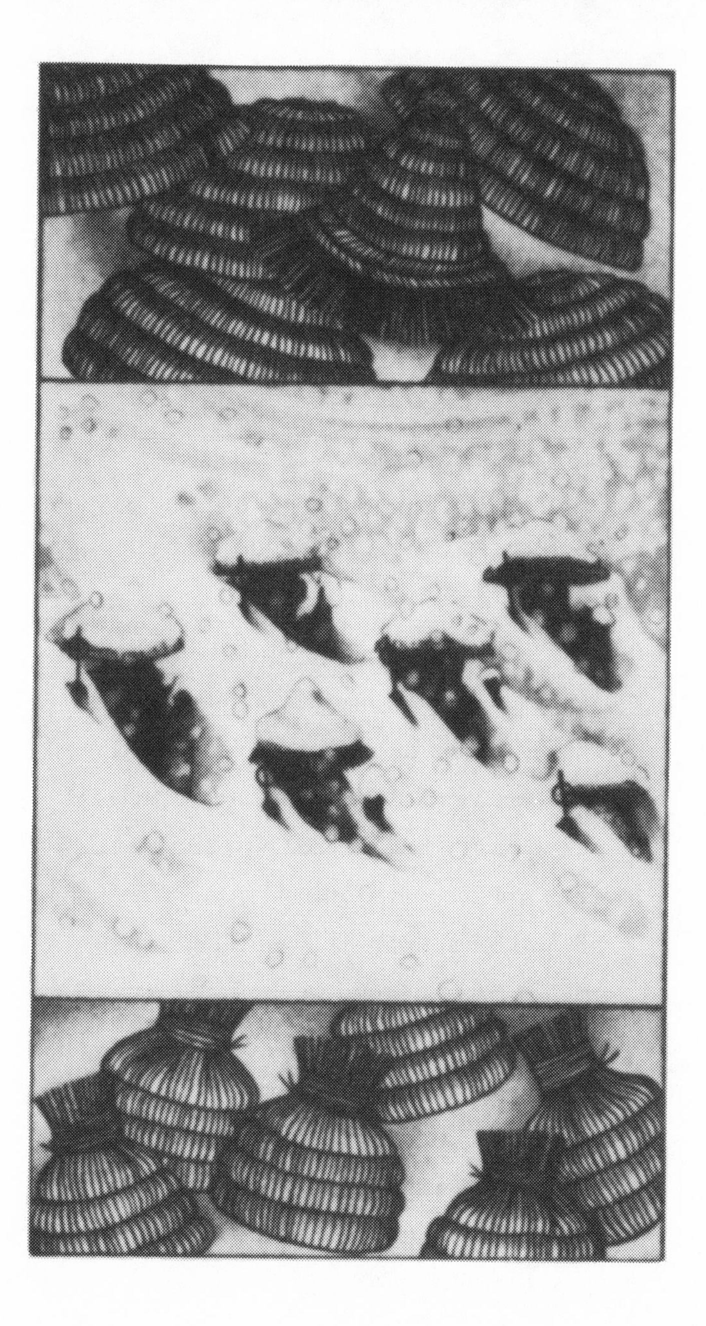

"*Yoi-sah! Hoi-sah! Yoi-sah! Hoi-sah!*" they called as they drew nearer and nearer.

"They seem to be coming here!" the old man gasped in amazement. But the old woman was too surprised even to speak.

As they watched, each of the Jizo statues came up to their house and left his sack at the doorstep.

The old man hurried to open the door, and as he did, the six big sacks came tumbling inside. In the sacks the old man and woman found rice and wheat, fish and beans, wine and bean paste cakes, and all sorts of delicious things that they might want to eat.

"Why, there is enough here for a feast every day all during the year!" the old man cried excitedly.

"And we shall have the finest New Year's feast we have ever had in our lives," the old woman exclaimed.

"Ojizo Sama, thank you!" the old man shouted.

"Ojizo Sama, how can we thank you enough?" the old woman called out.

But the six stone statues were already moving slowly down the road, and as the old man and woman watched, they disappeared into the whiteness of the falling snow, leaving only their footprints to show that they had been there at all.

GOMBEI AND THE WILD DUCKS

Once long ago, in a small village in Japan, there lived a man whose name was Gombei. He lived very close to a wooded marsh where wild ducks came each winter to play in the water for many long hours. Even when the wind was cold and the marsh waters were frozen, the ducks came in great clusters, for they liked Gombei's marsh, and they often stayed to sleep on the ice.

Just as his father had done before him, Gombei made his living by trapping the wild ducks with simple loops of rope. When a duck stepped into a loop, Gombei simply pulled the rope tight and the duck was caught. And like his father before him, Gombei never trapped more than one duck each day.

"After all, the poor creatures come to the marsh never suspecting that they will be caught," Gombei's father had said. "It would be too cruel to trap more than one at a time."

And so for all the years that Gombei trapped, he never caught more than one duck a day.

One cold winter morning, however, Gombei woke up with a dreary ache in his bones. "I am growing too old to work so hard, and there is no reason to continue as my father did for so many years," he said to himself. "If I caught one hundred ducks all at once, I could loaf for ninety-nine days without working at all."

Gombei wondered why he hadn't done this sooner. "It is a brilliant idea," he thought.

The very next morning, he hurried out to the marsh and discovered that its waters were frozen. "Very good! A fine day for trapping," he murmured, and quickly he laid a hundred traps on the icy surface. The sun had not yet come up and the sky was full of dark clouds. Gombei knelt behind a tree and clutched the ends of the hundred rope traps as he shivered and waited for the ducks to come.

Slowly the sky grew lighter and Gombei could see some ducks flying toward his marsh. He held his breath and watched eagerly as they swooped down onto the ice. They did not see his traps at all and gabbled noisily as they searched for food. One by one as the ducks stepped into his traps, Gombei tightened his hold on the ropes.

"One— two— three—" he counted, and in no time at all, he had ninety-nine ducks in his traps. The day had not even dawned and already his work was done for the next ninety-nine days. Gombei grinned at his cleverness and thought of the days and weeks ahead during which he could loaf.

"One more," he said patiently, "just one more duck and I will have a hundred."

The last duck, however, was the hardest of all to catch. Gombei waited and waited, but still there was no duck in his last trap. Soon the sky grew bright for the sun had appeared at the rim of the wooded hills, and suddenly a shaft of light scattered a rainbow of sparkling colors over the ice. The startled ducks uttered a shrill cry and almost as one they fluttered up into the sky, each trailing a length of rope from its legs.

Gombei was so startled by their sudden flight, he didn't let go of the ropes he held in his hands. Before he could even call for help, he found himself swooshed up into the cold winter sky as the ninety-nine wild ducks soared upward, pulling him along at the end of their traps.

"Stop! Let me down!" Gombei shouted, but the ducks soared on and on. Higher and higher they flew, over rivers and fields and hills, and beyond distant villages that Gombei had never seen before.

"Help! Save me!" Gombei called frantically, but there was no one to hear him high up in the sky.

Gombei was so frightened his face turned white and then green, but all he could do was hold on with all his strength to the ninety-nine pieces of rope. If he let go now, all would be over. He glanced down and then quickly clamped his eyes shut. The land below was whirling about like a toy top.

"Somebody! Help!" he shouted once more, but the only sound that came back to him was the steady flap-flap, flap-flap of the wild ducks' wings.

Soon one hand began to slip, a little at first, and then a little more. He was losing his grip on the ropes! Slowly Gombei felt the ropes slide from his numb fingers and finally, he was unable to hold on any longer. He closed his eyes tight and murmured a quick prayer as he plummeted pell-mell down to earth. The wild ducks, not knowing what had happened, flew on trailing their ropes behind like ribbons in the sky.

As Gombei tumbled toward the ground, however,

a very strange thing began to take place. First, he sprouted a bill, and then feathers and wings, and then a tail and webbed feet. By the time he was almost down to earth, he looked just like the creatures he had been trying to trap. Gombei wondered if he were having a bad dream. But no, he was flying and flapping his wings, and when he tried to call out, the only sound that came from him was the call of the wild duck. He had indeed become a wild duck himself. Gombei fluttered about frantically, trying to think and feel like a duck instead of a man. At last, he decided there was only one thing to do.

"If I am to be a wild duck, I must live like one," he thought, and he headed slowly toward the waters of a marsh he saw glistening in the sun. He was so hungry he simply had to find something to eat, for he had not even had breakfast yet. He swooped down to the marsh and looked about hungrily. But as he waddled about thinking only of his empty stomach, he suddenly felt a tug at his leg. He pulled and he pulled, but he could not get away. Then he looked down, and there wound around his leg was the very same kind of rope trap that he set each day for the wild ducks of his marsh.

"I wasn't harming anything. All I wanted was some food," he cried. But the man who had set the trap could not understand what Gombei was trying to say. He had been trapped like a wild animal and soon he would be plucked and eaten.

"Oh-h-h-h me," Gombei wailed, "now I know how terrible it is for even one wild duck to be trapped, and only this morning I was trying to trap a hundred poor birds. I am a wicked and greedy man," he thought, "and I deserve to be punished for being so cruel."

As Gombei wept, the tears trickled down his body and touched the rope that was wound tightly about his leg. The moment they did, a wonderful thing happened. The rope that was so secure suddenly fell apart and Gombei was no longer caught in the trap.

"I'm free! I'm free!" Gombei shouted, and this time he wept tears of joy. "How good it is to be free and alive! How grateful I am to have another chance," he cried.

As the tears rolled down his face, and then his body, another strange and marvelous thing happened. First, his feathers began to disappear, and then his bill, and then his tail and his webbed feet. Finally he was no longer a duck, but had become a human being once more.

"I'm not a duck! I'm a man again," Gombei called out gleefully. He felt his arms to be sure they were no longer wings. Yes, there were his fingers and his hands. He felt his nose to be sure it was no longer a duck's bill and he looked down in astonishment at the clothes that had reappeared on his body. Then he ran down the road as fast as his two human legs would carry him, and hurried home to his own village by the wooded marsh.

"Never again will I ever trap another living thing," Gombei vowed when he reached home safely. Then he went to his cupboard and threw out all his rope traps and burned them into ash.

"From this moment on, I shall become a farmer," he said. "I will till the soil and grow rice and wheat and food for all the living creatures of the land." And Gombei did exactly that for the rest of his days.

As for the wild ducks, they came in ever-increasing numbers, for now they found grain and feed instead of traps laid upon the ice, and they knew that in the sheltered waters of Gombei's marsh they would always be safe.

THE WONDERFUL TALKING BOWL

Long ago in a faraway village, there lived a farmer with his three sons, Taro, Jiro and Goro. Each day, from early morning until the sun had set, the three boys worked hard in their father's fields, planting, weeding and harvesting the crops.

One day, however, the farmer decided that his boys should learn something other than farming. He called them together and said, "My sons, you may each leave home for three years to do as you wish. The only thing I ask is that you learn a new skill. To the one who returns with the finest accomplishment, I shall give the house and all the land."

Immediately the boys made plans for their three years of freedom.

"I shall become an expert archer," Taro thought. "Then I shall be able to hunt the fields and forests and bring the finest game of the countryside to our table. Surely that would be a fine skill to possess."

The second son, Jiro, had still another idea. "I shall learn how to make things with my hands," he decided. "I shall learn to weave the hats worn by the nobles of the land, for that is a well-respected skill that only a few can master."

So Taro and Jiro quickly left their father's home in search of the finest teachers they could find.

Goro, the youngest, also left the house eagerly, but he had no idea at all what he would do with his three years. First he wandered through the fields, feeling the warmth of the sun on his back. Then he roamed through forests of pine and cedar, breathing deeply of the fresh cool mountain air. He walked and he walked, feeling free and content. But before long, the shadows of evening spun about him and he realized that he still had not decided what new skill he might learn.

Soon he saw a small, thatch-roofed farmhouse in a clearing at the edge of the forest. It was old and run-down, but it would provide shelter for the night. Goro knocked on the door and an old withered woman appeared to greet him.

"Come in, traveler, and take a rest," she said. "The sun has set and the night will be cold." She welcomed Goro into her small house and shared with him her meager meal of rice and turnips and salt fish.

"You are very kind," Goro said gratefully. And while they ate, he told her of his father's proposal.

"It is a fine thing to have three years of freedom, but I do not know what to do with myself," he explained. "Perhaps you could tell me how to make something of myself so I might win my father's house and land."

The old woman laughed a wisp of a laugh and shook her gray head. "Now what could I possibly say to help you with a problem like that?" she asked. "I am only a poor and tired old woman barely able to keep myself alive."

"I can offer you a quilt to spread on the floor, however," she added, and she told Goro that he was welcome to spend the night in her home. "Perhaps by morning you will think of what you can do with your three years," she said, and then she left him to think alone in the darkness.

All night long, thoughts tumbled about in Goro's head, but there was not a single good idea among them.

When the hazy light of morning sifted down through the trees of the forest, his mind was still as empty as it had been the day before.

"What shall I do with myself, old woman?" Goro asked once more.

"Well, if you have nothing better to do," she answered at last, "why don't you stay and help me for a while? I am alone and need help in the fields. I could use a strong young arm, and in return, I shall cook and wash for you."

Goro was too good-hearted to refuse. After all, the old woman had been kind to him on his first night away from home. Surely he could help her for a while.

"All right, old woman," he said gently. "I have three years and I am willing to take some time to help you out."

From the very next morning, Goro arose each day at dawn and worked until nightfall. He kept the old woman's rice fields growing full and green in the spring, and harvested them when they grew golden in the fall. He planted winter wheat and helped her grind flour. He helped her collect kindling and chopped wood for her fire. He worked harder than he had ever worked at home, and he felt happy and content.

Many months passed, and one day, Goro realized that his three years were almost gone and he still had learned nothing new. He hurried to the old woman saying, "I must be on my way now, good friend, for the many months I have spent here will soon become three years."

The old woman nodded and did not try to stop him. "You have helped me well and I shall always be grateful," she said. "Without you, I might have starved to death two winters ago."

Then she went to her cupboard and from a wooden box on the top shelf, she took out an old cracked lacquer bowl.

"I have nothing of great value to give you," she said slowly, "but please take this bowl as a farewell gift. Perhaps someday, it will bring you good fortune."

The old woman wiped the bowl with the sleeve of her *kimono* and gave it to Goro as though it were a very precious thing.

"Thank you, old woman," Goro said, and then, bidding her goodbye, he put the bowl in his sleeve and set off for home.

As he walked through the dew-covered grass, however, Goro felt a rumbling in his heart. What had he accomplished in three long years? He had done nothing better than he would have done at home. He hadn't learned a single new skill, and all the thanks he got for his hard work was an old cracked bowl. The more Goro thought of this, the angrier he became. He felt the bowl bumping about in his sleeve and finally, in a fit of anger, he took it out and flung it to the ground. Then he walked on.

Soon he heard a small, high voice. "Wait for me, Goro San!" it called. "Wait for me!"

Goro looked around, but saw no one. He took a few more steps when he heard the same little voice again. "Wait, wait! Please wait for me!" it begged.

Once more Goro looked around. There was no one in sight, but there on the ground, he saw the cracked bowl rolling and bumping along toward him. It rolled over rocks and over clumps of grass and finally it hopped up into his sleeve.

"Hmmm, you are a strange bowl indeed," Goro mused. "But since you have followed me this far, I suppose I should take you along."

So Goro walked on and on. Soon the sun grew hot and he stopped beside a mountain spring. "I might as well use the bowl since it is in my sleeve," he thought, and he used it to scoop up the cool spring water. When he had had enough, he threw the bowl aside and hurried on.

But he had taken only a few steps when the bowl called to him again. "Wait for me, Goro San! Wait for me!" And once more it rolled over the ground and hopped right into his sleeve. There was nothing to do but to take it along.

"Well, I have accomplished nothing in three years," Goro said ruefully, "but I have acquired a talking bowl and surely my brothers will possess nothing like that."

After many days, Goro and his cracked bowl finally reached home. There, he found his father and uncle waiting for him. His two brothers had already arrived and were also waiting for Goro so each could tell of his accomplishments.

"Well, Taro," the father asked, "what have you done with your three years?"

In reply Taro took a slim bow and arrow and aimed at a pear tree several hundred yards away. An arrow whizzed into the air and as it struck its mark, the ripest, most beautiful pear on the tree fell to the ground.

The father and uncle clapped their hands in approval. "Well done, my son," the father said. "You are an expert archer and that is an accomplishment to be proud of!"

Next it was Jiro's turn. From two large baskets he produced an armful of beautiful hats woven for the nobility of the land. They were so light and graceful, even the Weaver Goddess could have done no better.

"An excellent accomplishment, my son," the father commended. "You will never go hungry if you can provide our nobles with such hats as these!"

Then, at last, the father turned to Goro. "And you, my son?" he asked. "What is it that you have learned to do?"

Goro fidgeted nervously and looked at his feet. How could he possibly tell his father that he had learned nothing at all? Suddenly, he heard a small voice from his sleeve. "Tell him you have learned to steal," it urged.

And that is exactly what Goro found himself doing. "Father, I have learned to steal," he said boldly.

His father could not believe his ears. "What?" he exclaimed. "You have learned to steal?"

"Surely, you must be joking," his brothers cried.

But Goro went on. "It is true," he said. "That is all I learned to do in the three years I have been away."

Now his uncle who had been listening carefully, turned to Goro. "Well, perhaps stealing is an accomplishment too, if you can do it well." Then, with a sly smile, he spoke of a plan.

"Listen well, Goro," he said. "If you can enter my house tonight and steal my money boxes, I shall give you all the gold they contain. However, if you are caught, I shall send you to jail to rot like a common thief. Do you agree to this plan?"

"But—but Uncle—" Goro began. He was about to confess that he could not steal a penny from a blind beggar when once again the bowl spoke to him. "Go ahead, do as he says!" it urged.

Goro cleared his throat. "Very well then, Uncle," he said. "I accept your challenge. I shall steal your money boxes this very night."

Goro sounded brave, but deep inside, he knew he could never succeed and that he would probably find himself in jail. Not only had he wasted three years, he had acquired a bowl that did nothing but cause him trouble. Goro was miserable.

His uncle, on the other hand, felt very clever. He knew, too, that Goro would not succeed, and he intended to teach him a lesson by throwing him in jail.

That night a great storm swept in from the sea, and it rained as though the river of heaven had burst its banks. The uncle locked his house carefully and instructed his servants.

"Keep your flint sticks close at hand and be ready to strike a light the moment I call out," he warned. Then he went to the stable and told the watchman to beware of thieves. When he had spoken to everyone, he waited for Goro to come.

In the driving rain, Goro plodded slowly to his uncle's house, holding an umbrella in one hand and clutching his cracked bowl in the other. As he stood wet and discouraged outside his uncle's gate, his uncle heard the sound of rain falling on Goro's big umbrella.

"The silly fool has come to rob me with an umbrella in his hand," he laughed, and because he felt sure Goro could not break in, the uncle went to bed.

"Now what am I to do?" Goro wondered dismally.

"Find a small opening and push me in!" the bowl called. "I will help you."

Goro soon found a crack in the walls and pushed the bowl inside. The moment it was in the house, the bowl sprouted a head and then two arms and legs, and it ran to the servants' quarters. Quickly it gathered up all the flint sticks and left pipes and flutes instead. Then, it dashed into the uncle's room and tied him up with his own sash.

"Help! Help!" the uncle shouted. "Strike the flint sticks! Light the lamps! Thief! Thief!"

The servants ran for the flint sticks, but they found only pipes and flutes. They tried to light fires with them, but all they produced were feeble squeaks and squawks. Everyone dashed about wildly, bumping into each other in the darkness, and soon the whole house was in an uproar.

Hearing the commotion, the stablehand ran into the house. "The money boxes! The money boxes!" the uncle called frantically.

"Yes, sir," the stablehand shouted, and thinking the uncle wanted to ride away with the boxes, he tied them to one of the horses and led it to the front gate.

However, it was not the uncle who rode off on the horse at all, for it was Goro who stood at the gate. Goro grabbed the reins from the startled stablehand,

leaped on the horse, and rode off with the money boxes tied securely to the saddle. With the help of his bowl, he had succeeded in robbing his uncle after all.

When the uncle discovered what had happened, he kept his promise and gave Goro all the gold in his money boxes. "I trust, however," he added, "that you will never steal again."

Goro could keep silent no longer. He admitted to his father and his uncle that he had never really learned to steal at all. He told how he helped an old woman for three years and about her strange and wonderful bowl.

"Your brothers will share my house and fields for the fine skills they learned," Goro's father said. "But the gift from the old woman has brought you an equally fine reward."

"It has indeed," Goro agreed, for the gold from his uncle had made him a wealthy man and he would be able to build a fine new home for himself.

He knew now that the old woman had more than repaid him for his three years of work and the bowl she had given him was truly a precious possession. It had brought him every measure of the good fortune she had wished for him and a great deal more.

THE TERRIBLE BLACK SNAKE'S REVENGE

High in a small mountain village, there once lived a man whose name was Badger. One day Badger had to go to the village on the other side of the mountains, and in order to do that, he had to travel through a deep and dark forest. The mountain forest was full of bears and wolves and snakes that hid in the tall grass, and Badger trembled as he thought about them.

"Be especially careful of the terrible Black Snake of the Mountains," the villagers warned, "for if he catches you, he will swallow you alive and we will never see you again."

"I know, I know," Badger answered weakly, and his knees wobbled at the very thought of this monstrous snake.

Before dawn the next morning, Badger set out so that he would be clear of the forest by nightfall. He walked briskly into the mountains, whistling to keep up his spirits. Soon he was tramping along the narrow path deep in the shadowy woods, trying hard not to think of the fearful snake. He walked and he walked and he walked, but no matter how far he went, he couldn't seem to get over the mountains. He looked up at the sky and saw the sun creeping higher and higher over his head. Soon it began to dip beyond the treetops and still Badger had not gotten out of the mountain forest. Before long, the dusky shadows of nightfall were all about him and poor Badger knew that he had lost his way.

"Of all the dreadful terrible places to be lost," he muttered, shuddering as he thought of what the night would bring. But it was useless to roam any longer. "I must find a safe place to spend the night," he thought, and he looked about for a good hiding place.

At last he came upon a deep cave sheltered behind a mass of boulders. "Ah, this will do nicely until morning," Badger thought, and he quickly crawled inside and tried to sleep.

As the night wore on, the wind shrieked and moaned, and the trees of the forest seemed to whisper and sigh like a gathering of sorrowful ghosts. An owl hooted dismally above his head and somewhere in the distant hills a wolf was howling at the moon. Badger closed his eyes tight and tried not to hear the night sounds of the forest, but it was impossible for him to sleep.

About midnight he heard a strange sound. At first it was a faint rustle and then it came closer and closer and closer. Badger shrank into the corner of the cave scarcely daring to breathe. And then something appeared at the mouth of the cave and Badger saw a dark shadow moving inside. It was something long and black and slippery. It was the terrible Black Snake of the Mountains himself, and he slithered closer and closer and closer!

Badger tried to call for help. His mouth was open, but not a sound came out. Frantically, he looked about for a stone or a stick, for if he did not strike the snake first, he would surely be swallowed alive. As he fumbled about desperately, the snake suddenly stopped and spoke to him.

"Who are you and what are you doing in my cave?" he asked quite politely.

"M-m-m-my n-n-n-name—" Poor Badger was so terrified he could not speak. Finally, he simply stuttered, "B-b-b-badger!"

The snake hissed a snake-like laugh. "Ah, so you are a badger," he said. "For a moment I thought you were a human being. You have surely turned yourself into a very good imitation of a human being."

And the snake, believing that he was talking to another animal, relaxed and curled himself into a nice round coil.

"I have heard that you badgers are very clever at disguising yourselves," he said almost enviously. "Now I have seen for myself how well you do."

The snake talked on and on, for he did not have many friends, and furthermore they did not usually come to share his cave in the middle of the night. He told Badger of all the villagers he had swallowed and how delicious they had been.

"They are very frightened of me, I hear," he said boastfully. Then he turned to Badger and asked, "Tell me, is there anything at all that you are truly afraid of?"

Badger almost stammered, "You!" But of course he could never say that. "Well," he said thoughtfully, "I hear that gold is a very cursed thing and that it can very well ruin one. I suppose the thing I fear most is gold."

The snake nodded his big black head and then, because he believed he was talking to a friend, he said, "If you promise never to tell anyone, I will tell you what I fear the most."

"I promise," Badger replied. "Tell me what it is."

"Well," said the snake, writhing at the thought, "what frightens me most is hot melted tar. I could very well be trapped and killed with it." Then the snake stopped and looked straight into Badger's eyes. "If you tell anyone what I have just told you, I will find you no matter where you are and I will seek a fearful revenge. Do you understand?"

Once more Badger was too frightened to speak. He simply nodded his head and wished with all his heart that he were back home in his village.

At last the sun began to rise, and when a streak of light burst into the cave, the snake slithered off, muttering, "I must find another place of darkness until midnight."

Badger gave up all thought of doing any business in the village beyond the mountains. He somehow found his way out of the forest and ran back to his village like a mouse running from a cat. He sputtered out his story of spending the night in the dark cave with the terrible Black Snake of the Mountains. "And I have discovered what it is that the snake fears the most!" he burst out. "Now we can kill him and no one need ever be afraid of crossing the mountains again."

"Badger, you are a brave man!" the villagers cried. And that very night, Badger led them into the forest with a tub full of hot melted tar. They hid behind the boulders beside the cave and waited silently in the black-velvet forest night. About midnight they finally heard the Black Snake moving over the leaves. The moment he entered his cave they leaped out, and with a great shout they poured in the hot melted tar.

"Never again will you swallow up our villagers!" they cried angrily.

The snake let out a great hissing sound, but he was very clever and very quick, and he somehow escaped the hot melted tar. He managed to slip out of the cave and disappeared into a deep mountain pool before any of the villagers could catch him.

"We have missed our chance," Badger said desolately. "We didn't kill the Black Snake after all." And they all returned to the village feeling anxious and disappointed.

But of all the villagers, Badger was more frightened than anyone else, for he remembered the snake's last words to him. "Now he will surely come to find me and seek revenge," Badger thought miserably, and he wondered what terrible fate awaited him that night.

He bolted his door and pushed a great heavy charcoal brazier in front of it. He tried to sleep, but he was much too frightened for that, so he sat before the hearth and waited as the night grew cold and still. Then, at last, toward midnight, he heard a sound outside.

"He has found me already," Badger said with a shiver.

Now there was a rustling at the window, and soon the terrible Black Snake thrust his big black head inside.

"You traitor!" he hissed. "You not only lied to me, you broke your promise and you even tried to kill me. I have come to punish you with a basketful of the one thing you fear most!"

And with a great clatter and crash he threw in an enormous basket that was filled with gold coins.

"Now I have been avenged," the snake hissed and he quickly disappeared into the darkness.

Badger blinked hard and looked at all the gold that was strewn about his floor. Then when he realized what had happened, he threw back his head and laughed until the tears rolled down his cheeks. He had not only fooled the Black Snake, he had become a wealthy man.

The snake soon discovered that he had been deceived, and grew so angry and embarrassed that he disappeared completely from the mountains and never swallowed another human being again. The mountains and forest became safe once more, and Badger lived a good and long life with all the gold he received from the terrible Black Snake.

KOICHI AND THE MOUNTAIN GOD

Long, long ago, there lived a poor widow and her only child, a boy whose name was Koichi. For many years the mother had struggled all alone to raise her son, but now at last he was sixteen.

"Mother, you have worked long and hard," he said. "Now let me do the work and take care of you."

So Koichi went to the mountains each day to cut wood, just as his father had done, and each day his mother packed a delicious lunch for him to take along.

One day when Koichi went into the woods, he hung his lunch on a low branch of a tall pine and climbed the tree to cut some of the higher limbs. In a little while he looked down and saw an old white-haired man hobbling toward his tree. The old man looked at Koichi's lunch, took it down, and without even looking for its owner, proceeded to eat it up.

"That's strange," Koichi thought. "The poor man must be very hungry to eat my lunch."

He did not mind too much, however, for he knew his mother would have a good dinner for him that night, with plenty of freshly cooked rice. He climbed down the tree and said, "I'm glad you enjoyed my lunch, old man."

The old man did not even seem surprised or embarrassed. He simply said, "I was terribly hungry and your lunch was very good. *Arigato.* My thanks to you."

When Koichi got home that night, he told his mother of the strange old man.

After she had heard the story, she nodded with approval and said, "I'm glad you let a hungry old man have your lunch. Tomorrow I will make an extra lunch for him as well."

So the next day Koichi took two lunches with him to the woods. Again he hung his bundle containing the lunches on a low limb and climbed up to cut some of the higher branches. Soon the old man appeared once more. Without even bothering to look for Koichi, he simply took down the bundle as though it belonged to him. Then he sat down and calmly ate not only one, but both lunches.

"What a strange thing to do," Koichi thought. "Surely he must have known one of those lunches was for me."

Still, he felt sorry for the old man who probably had nothing at home to eat. He decided not to say anything unkind, and when he climbed down the tree, he simply said, "Old man, I'm glad you enjoyed both lunches."

"Ah yes," the old man answered. "I worked hard today and I was very hungry indeed. You are most kind." Then, when he had finished eating, he disappeared into the woods.

The next day the very same thing happened again, but this time the old man did not vanish. He sat down beside Koichi and said, "Young man, you have been kind and generous to me, and now I shall tell you who I am. I am the God of the Mountains, so listen carefully to what I say."

Koichi knelt beside the old man and listened with his whole being.

"Go home and prepare yourself for a trip to

Tenjiku," the Mountain God told him. "There you will find the most beautiful temple in all of Japan. Before you reach it, however, you will meet some people who will ask you to do something for them. Be as kind to them as you were to me, and you can be sure good fortune will come to you."

Koichi opened his mouth to ask the old man some questions. But before he could utter a word, the Mountain God was gone, and in his place stood a great, gnarled oak tree. Koichi couldn't wait to finish his day's work. He ran home and quickly told his mother what had happened.

"This is a wonderful thing," she said joyfully. "You must do exactly as the God of the Mountains directed." And she set to work preparing for his journey.

Koichi's mother knew, however, that it would be a long trip over the western hills to Tenjiku and she did not have enough money to buy all that he would need. She decided at last to go to the wealthiest man of the village and ask if she might borrow some food and money for Koichi's great journey.

When he heard the story of the Mountain God, he was eager to help. "Of course, of course," he agreed.

"Just ask your son to pray for my daughter when he reaches the temple and learn how she might be cured of the illness that has claimed her for three years."

"That is an easy task indeed," Koichi said when he learned of the wealthy man's request. "I shall not forget to pray for his daughter and ask how she might be cured."

In a few days, his mother had prepared a bundle of food and clothing, and Koichi was ready to leave. With the rising sun behind him and his mother's blessings to protect him, he began his long trip. He walked and walked for days and days, crossing mountains and forests and passing field after field of fresh green rice. Then one day he came to a village where he passed a magnificent mansion. At the massive wooden gate of the mansion stood the master of the house.

"Where are you going, young traveler?" the master asked.

"To the temple at Tenjiku," Koichi replied.

The man immediately stopped him and asked if he would do something for him. "When you reach the temple, will you learn why only one of my three cherry trees ever blooms in the spring? In return, I shall give you a night's lodging in my home."

"Of course," Koichi answered. "That is an easy task." So he spent the night at the beautiful mansion and early the next morning he hurried on toward Tenjiku.

As he walked along, he soon came to a wild and rushing river. He looked up and down, but there was neither a bridge nor a boat by which he could cross.

"I can't let a river stop me after I have come this far," Koichi thought, and he looked about for some help. As he did, he saw a wraith-like woman standing on the opposite bank, her face hidden behind her long black hair.

"Excuse me," he called out to her. "Could you tell me how I might get across this river?"

Suddenly the woman skimmed over to him, floating over the water's surface like a pale ghost. "Where are you going, my child?" she asked in a shivery blue voice.

"To Tenjiku," Koichi answered. "To the most beautiful temple in all the world."

"Ah, if that is where you are going, will you do something for me?" she asked in a thin wail. "For a thousand years I have lived on the river's mist and the ocean's spray—neither alive nor dead. Please find out how I can get to heaven and find some peace."

"Of course I will," Koichi replied. "That will be an easy task, and I will not forget."

"Then climb upon my shoulders," the ghostly woman instructed, and before Koichi knew what was happening, she had carried him to the other side of the river in a cloud of gray mist.

"Thank you," Koichi began, but the woman was gone.

When he looked up, he saw looming before him the resplendent grandeur of the Tenjiku temple. It soared to the sky at the top of eight hundred stone steps with thousands of straight tall pine trees lining the way. Its golden roof glittered and shimmered in the sun, and Koichi fell to his knees at the splendor of the sight. At that very moment, the God of the Mountains appeared once more before him.

"So, my son, you have come at last," he said. "You have traveled far, and did you not meet some people along the way who asked for your help?"

"I did indeed," Koichi replied, and he told the god about the young girl who could not be cured, the two cherry trees that would not bloom, and the ghostly woman who wanted to go to heaven.

"What can I tell them when I return?" he asked.

The God of the Mountains told Koichi to sit down. "Now listen carefully," he said. "Tell the father of the sick girl to gather before her all the young men of the neighborhood and put in her hand a cup of wine. The one to whom she gives the cup should become her husband and receive half of her father's wealth. When she selects the right young man, she will become healthy again."

Koichi nodded. "I will tell him," he said.

"Now for your second friend," the god continued. "Two pots of gold lie buried at the roots of the trees that do not bloom. Tell him to dig them up and give one away. From that very moment, his trees will blossom as though it were spring."

Again Koichi nodded. "I shall remember," he promised.

"As for the woman by the river," the god went on, "look in her right hand and you will find a golden ball. Tell her to give it away and in the flash of a swallow's wing, she will be able to go to heaven."

"I have heard you well," Koichi said. He bowed low to thank the god and when he looked up, a giant old oak tree stood where the god had been. No one

else lingered in the pocket of stillness that surrounded the temple and only a nightingale's faint song floated high up in the wooded hills.

Koichi climbed slowly up the eight hundred steps to the temple. There he burned some incense and murmured a prayer of thanks for the blessings of a safe journey. He remembered to pray for the sick daughter and for his mother who waited for him. Then he turned to begin the long journey home.

Retracing his steps, Koichi first came to the wraith of a woman who had lived for a thousand years. He told her what the god had said and immediately she produced a small golden ball from her right hand and gave it to Koichi.

"Keep it, young friend," she said. "It is yours."

The moment she spoke, a sound like the fluttering of a thousand wings filled the valley. As Koichi watched, a magnificent golden bridge slowly descended from the skies and the woman climbed upon it, vanishing into a silver cloud that would take her to heaven at last. Koichi smiled happily and put the golden ball into his bundle.

Next he came to the beautiful mansion where the master of the house waited eagerly for him.

"What news do you have for me?" he asked anxiously.

When Koichi told him what the god had said, the man dug near the roots of his trees and two pots of gold appeared just as the god had said. The man gave one to Koichi saying, "Here, my son, take this and keep it, for it belongs to you." And the moment he did, his two trees burst into glorious bloom filling the air with the sweetness of spring.

"It is exactly as the god said it would be," Koichi murmured, and a great happiness filled his heart.

Koichi hurried on with his golden ball and his pot of gold, and finally after many days, he reached his own home. In a great rush of words, he told his mother of his remarkable journey and then he hurried to the home of the wealthy man to tell him what the god had said.

Immediately the wealthy man gathered the young men of the neighborhood and gave his daughter a cup of wine. But the daughter shook her head and would not give the cup to anyone.

The wealthy man sent for Koichi and asked what was wrong. "I have done exactly as you said," he explained, "but my daughter does not offer the cup of wine to anyone, and she does not improve at all."

As Koichi came near, however, the daughter smiled, and it was to him that she finally offered the cup of wine. The moment she did, her cheeks grew pink and her strength returned. "I am well, Father," she said, weeping with joy. "I am truly well at last!"

"The Mountain God spoke the truth indeed," Koichi said. "Truly good things have come to me and this is the greatest of my joys."

And so it was that Koichi was chosen to become the daughter's husband and to receive half of her father's wealth. When the time came at length for them to marry, Koichi first built his mother a fine new home. Then with his beautiful young bride, he lived a life of great happiness and contentment. Whenever he walked among the silent trees of the forest he hoped the God of the Mountains might appear before him, but never again did he see the old man or the mighty gnarled oak. All that remained of his wonderful journey was the memory of the golden temple soaring above the hills of Tenjiku and the song of the forest nightingale that foretold his great good fortune.

GLOSSARY

arigato	*ah-ree-gah-toh*	thank you
furoshiki	*foo-roh-shee-kee*	a square cloth for wrapping and carrying small articles
Gombei	*Gohm-bay*	
Goro San	*Goh-roh Sahn*	Mr. Goro
Higa	*Hee-gah*	
Hikoichi	*Hee-koh-ee-chee*	
Ise	*Ee-seh*	
Jiro	*Jee-roh*	
Jizo	*Jee-zoh*	the guardian god of children
Kentsu San	*Ken-tsoo Sahn*	Mr. Kentsu
kimono	*kee-moh-noh*	a Japanese dress
Koichi	*Koh-ee-chee*	
Kotaro	*Koh-tah-roh*	
mah mah	*mah-mah*	"My, my"
oi	*oi*	"Hey!"
Ojizo Sama	*Oh-jee-zoh Sah-mah*	polite form of Jizo
Osaka	*Oh-sah-kah*	
Roku	*Roh-koo*	
sah sah	*sah-sah*	"Come, come"
sayonara	*sah-yoh-nah-rah*	goodbye
Taro	*Tah-roh*	
tengu	*ten-goo*	a long-nosed goblin

Tenjiku	*Ten-jee-koo*	
yare yare	*yah-ray yah-ray*	"Ah ah" or "Ah me"
Yoi-sah! Hoi-sah!	*yoi-sah hoi-sah*	an exclamation, such as "heave ho!"

NOTE: *These words should be pronounced with equal stress on each syllable.*

Yoshiko Uchida was born in Alameda, California and grew up in Berkeley, the locale of her recent trilogy, *A Jar of Dreams*, *The Best Bad Thing* and *The Happiest Ending*. She earned her BA with honors from the University of California, Berkeley, and has a Masters in Education from Smith College.

She began writing when she was ten years old, creating small books out of brown wrapping paper in which to write her stories. She is now the author of twenty-five published books for young people and has won many awards for her work, including a Distinguished Service Award from the University of Oregon.

Her published work for adults includes many articles and short stories as well as a novel, *Picture Bride*, and a non-fiction book, *Desert Exile*, which tells of her family's World War II internment experiences when they were among the 120,000 Japanese Americans imprisoned by the US government.

Although many of her earlier books were about Japan and its young people (including three collections of Japanese folk tales, *The Dancing Kettle*, *The Magic Listening Cap* and *The Sea of Gold*), her recent work focuses on the Japanese American experience in California.

She says of her work, "I hope to give young Asians a sense of their own history, but at the same time, I want to dispel the stereotypic image held by many non-Asians about the Japanese Americans and write about them as real people. I also want to convey the sense of hope and strength of spirit of the first generation Japanese Americans. Beyond that," she adds, "I want to celebrate our common humanity."